The
ME TOO
GIRL

Lance & James
MORCAN

Published by:

Sterling Gate Books

28 St. Heliers Pl.,

Papamoa 3118,

Bay of Plenty,

New Zealand

sterlinggatebooks@gmail.com

National Library of New Zealand publication data:

Morcan, Lance 1948-

Morcan, James 1978-

Title: The Me Too Girl

Edition: First ed.

Format: Paperback

Publisher: Sterling Gate Books

ISBN: 978-0-473-51973-5

Dedicated to abused women everywhere – and to those individuals (men and women) who help convict the abusers.

1

Susan Fox was lost in thought as the cab she traveled in negotiated the City of Angels' horrendous rush-hour traffic. Her destination was the *Sheraton Grand Hotel* in South Hope Street – the venue for a celebration of the recent re-election of Los Angeles' popular mayor, Dean Lopez.

Twenty-two-year-old Susan, or Suzie to friends and colleagues, was attending the function in her capacity as a member of the mayor's now disbanded election team of voluntary canvassers. That successful exercise, along with a glowing testimonial from an appreciative Mayor Lopez, had helped secure her a sought-after position as an account executive with a prestigious boutique public relations firm. It was her first job, her first real job, since graduating from UCLA where she excelled in the allied fields of communications and journalism.

When the cab stopped for a red light, Suzie reflected on the past week. It was, she thought, *the* week from hell. And that was saying something. As someone who had been subjected to sexual abuse throughout her teens, first by a guardian with pedophiliac predilections in Illinois and then by a sadistic predator in California, she'd had some bad times to contend with, but this past week, in her opinion, had to be one of the worst.

I was still buzzing when I approached my modest apartment complex in West 1st Street at the end of the first week in my new job at *Boutique PR*. In fact, it felt like I was walking on air. Not only had my first five days in the job confirmed I'd found my calling in life, but my manager had just today given me a new client to manage – a responsibility almost unheard of for a junior account executive with no public relations experience to speak of. An added bonus was that the firm's premises adjoined nearby Los Angeles City Hall so it was easy enough to walk to and from work rather than take an Uber ride or catch a bus. Consequently, I walked to and from work most days. I looked on it as part of my fitness routine.

Waiting to cross the busy street in the company of a dozen or so homeless citizens, who, I assumed, were residents of nearby Skid Row, I took no notice of the admiring glances of three suited businessmen also waiting. The attention of members of the opposite sex, both single and married, used to unsettle me, but I'd gotten used to it over the years. It was a case of having to, I guess. I wasn't planning to make myself any less attractive than I was, and men sure as hell weren't about to lose their predator instincts. Not this late in the evolutionary process.

Nor did I take any notice of the Los Angeles Police Department patrol car parked outside the entrance to my apartment complex. After all, the LAPD's headquarters were also located in West 1st Street and their patrol cars were a common sight in this vicinity. Nor did I pay any attention to the suited individual who occupied the patrol car's front passenger seat. Had I paid attention, I would have noticed he was observing me. I might also have recognized him, and that would have been cause for concern.

The first I became aware *he* was waiting for me was when I crossed the street. I was about to enter the building when the patrol car's passenger door opened and the passenger stepped out, blocking my path. I recognized him immediately despite the fact last time I saw him he wore the uniform of a police officer.

Holy shit!

2

Hector Williams, or Heck to his associates, was the LAPD's Deputy Chief of Police. He was also kind of hard to forget. A hulking specimen, the forty-nine-year-old Williams stood six foot six and towered over all but a rare few of the passersby currently using the sidewalk outside my apartment.

That wasn't the main reason I remembered Deputy Chief Williams, however. We had a history of sorts. A history I'd rather forget.

Williams smiled at me as he ran his eyes over my body and made no attempt to hide the fact he liked what he saw. His was a cruel smile and there was no affection in those cold, gray eyes.

Glancing at the security camera above the building's entrance, he smiled again as he flashed his ID card and, turning his face away from the camera, he said, "Hey little Suzie, remember me? I'm now Deputy Chief Hector Williams."

I shuddered involuntarily.

I remember you alright.

"What the hell do you want?"

"Now, is that any way to greet ol' Heck?"

Williams took me gently but firmly by the arm and escorted me a little way along the sidewalk. Whether it was because of the presence of the security camera or the close proximity of his fellow officer in the nearby patrol car I wasn't sure. Knowing him, it was probably because of both of those things.

As we walked, my mind was racing. When I'd last seen Williams I'd been using another name and residing elsewhere in this city – in Venice, to be precise. That was three or four years ago now. Since then, I'd adopted a complete change of lifestyle, reverted to using my real name and relocated to new premises at least three times. In doing so, I believed I'd never see the man again. At least I prayed I'd never see him again.

How in God's name did you find me, Hector?

Then it came to me…

3

A profile story on my addition to the staff of *Boutique PR* appeared mid-week under *New Appointments* in the business section of the *Los Angeles Times*. It included a two-column portrait photo of myself, and, if I had to bet, Williams spotted the photo.

Twenty yards or so further along the sidewalk he steered me into a narrow alley that ran alongside my apartment building, and only then did he stop and let go my arm. I saw we had the alley to ourselves for the moment.

All business now, the deputy chief immediately confirmed he'd seen the story on my appointment in the *Times* and said one phone call was all it had taken to find out where I lived.

"Ya kinda dropped off the grid there for a while, sweetheart," he said.

When I didn't respond, he added, "You and me have some unfinished business."

I had a feeling I knew where this was headed and I didn't like it. I didn't like it one bit.

"We have no unfinished business!" I shot back. "You're delusional!"

I turned to walk away, but he reached out and restrained me.

"I'd remind you I'm here on official police business… And I don't want to have to arrest you for obstruction."

Recovered from my initial shock, I said, "Bullshit! You're not here officially."

Pointing at the LAPD badge he wore beneath his suit jacket, Williams said, "This says I am."

He glared at me as if challenging me to dispute his claim.

Tall though I was, I felt dwarfed by the big cop. Williams was tall even by LAPD standards, and he was never slow to use his height to intimidate anyone who earned his displeasure. I could feel my earlier resolve dissipating.

"What do you want?" I asked.

"I have reason to believe you are still using illicit drugs–"

"What?"

"You heard me."

"There must be some mistake."

"No mistake I can assure you."

"I've put that life behind me!"

Williams pulled a face.

"You know what they say…Once a user always a user."

I didn't believe for one minute he thought I was still involved with drugs, but exactly what his game was I wasn't sure. It was about to become very clear very soon.

Williams asked, "Do they know about your past life?"

"Who?"

"Your employers at Boutique PR…Who else?"

"Of course they don't. My past is private."

"Until it catches up with you," Williams said. "How do ya think your employers would react if they learn you're a whore and a junkie?"

I could feel myself spiraling downwards into the depths of despair. This asshole was dragging up all the bad stuff in my former life. Stuff that I'd spent the last few years trying to forget. Stuff that I thought I'd successfully buried for good.

"I've told you already, that's all in the past!"

Looking at my shoulder bag, Williams said, "I want to search your bag."

"You need a search warrant to do that…and I don't see one."

"Well let's just pretend you agreed to let me search your bag," Williams sneered. Reaching into his suit trouser pocket, he pulled out an object, which he held up in front of my face. "And how do you explain this?"

I saw he was holding a clear plastic sachet containing what looked like white powder.

"Pure heroin," Williams said. "And what d'ya know? I found it hidden right here" – he pointed at my shoulder bag – "in your bag."

4

I stared aghast at the sachet, speechless.

We both remained quiet as a workman entered the alley. The man took no interest in us and passed us by.

"A Class A drug," Williams said as soon as the workman was out of earshot. Flicking the sachet with his finger, he added, "That's six months jail time right there."

"That doesn't belong to me!"

"Well, I say it does, Miss Fox."

It finally dawned on me the bastard was intent on framing me.

But why? What's there to gain?

As if reading my mind, Williams said, "Here's the deal. From now on bitch, you have an open door policy where I'm concerned, and whenever I feel the need for, uh, female companionship, you'll oblige me. Only this time you won't be charging me for your expert services."

I was shaking my head before he'd even finished.

"That's blackmail!"

Williams carried on undeterred.

"And in return, I will not only forget to file a crime report for this heroin I found on you today, but I won't mention your former career as a junkie and a hooker" – he smirked when he noticed me flinch at his choice of words – "to your current employers *or* to any *future* employers."

"I worked for a respectable escort agency as a confused teenager, as you well know, and I was never a junkie! I dabbled in drugs for a while…that's all!"

"You spread your legs for any fat bastard's money *and* you dabbled in hard drugs… heroin… And it was longer than a while. It was two years at least."

I could feel my whole world being turned upside down.

"You can't do this," I said.

Even to my ears I didn't sound convincing.

"We both know I can," Williams said.

I could feel the fight going out of me.

Stand up to him, Suzie!

"I'll report you!" I shouted.

"And who do you think they're gonna believe? You, with your previous track record, or me, a senior officer of the law?"

He flicked the sachet with his finger again as if to drive home his point.

"No!" I said, making a determined last stand. Hands on hips, I added,

"This is extortion!"

Williams grinned. It was a mirthless grin.

"Well, we can do this the hard way, then." Pulling his cellphone from his breast pocket, he said, "Why don't I call your employer at Boutique PR?"

He looked at me, awaiting a response.

The terrible sinking sensation I'd experienced earlier intensified. It almost felt as if I was drowning. The more I fought against it, the more desperate I felt. I could only imagine how much my reputation would suffer if my employer learned of my past involvement with drugs and prostitution.

Suddenly out of patience, Williams speed-dialed a number on his phone. Unless he was bluffing, he'd evidently stored my firm's number in his phone earlier.

"Let's see what your manager has to say, shall we?"

I could hear the phone ringing and I could feel my world crumbling as the big cop waited for a receptionist at *Boutique PR* to answer his call. I could only imagine what my manager and colleagues would think if all my dirty linen was publicly aired.

That would destroy me!

I couldn't stop the tears that were now running down my face.

In that moment I arrived at a terrible decision.

5

"Stop!" I said, holding out one hand imploringly.

Williams terminated the call before it was answered and looked back at me expectantly.

I was about to tell him what he wanted to hear when his fellow officer appeared at the end of the alley.

"Urgent message for you from HQ, sir," the uniformed officer said. "The chief wants to see you pronto."

Hiding his annoyance, Williams said, "I'll be right there."

He turned back to me, expecting to hear my answer.

Sensing the opportunity to stall, I said, "I need a week to think about it, Hector. Can you give me one week?"

Williams was about to remonstrate with me, but held off because his subordinate was still waiting.

"One week," he said. "No longer or I'll enforce the law…my law…in ways you won't like one little bit, little Suzie."

Without another word, he hurried off to join his subordinate who was already heading back to their waiting car.

The traffic light changed to green and the cab began inching forward once more, bringing Suzie back to the present.

Looking out the near window, she saw the traffic was now gridlocked.

Typical L.A.

She just hoped she wasn't going to be late for the mayoral function.

Thinking back on her unexpected encounter with Deputy Chief Williams she still couldn't get her head around it even though a week had elapsed since it occurred. The confrontation had turned her world upside down, revived memories she'd tried to forget and left her feeling confused, frightened and even disorientated at times.

After the reprieve Williams' subordinate had unwittingly given her in the alley, she'd hurried to the relative safety of her fifth floor apartment and spent the night going over everything her nemesis had said. Unfortunately for her, everything he'd said was true. She *had* been a drug addict and she *had* been involved in prostitution. What he hadn't acknowledged was that there were extenuating circumstances.

Formerly from Illinois, she had been sexually abused by her stepfather as a young teen. It seemed almost inevitable that she fell in with a bad crowd, took drugs to numb the pain, quit school and ran away from home. Arriving in L.A. with dreams of making it in Hollywood, she ended up totally messed up and intermittently living on the streets. Regular brushes with the law prompted her to change her name – to the unlikely *Gypsy Diamond*.

Gypsy, who was still only sixteen, came to the attention of a pimp, who, as a lucrative sideline, prospected beautiful girls with no family ties for an upmarket and unscrupulous escort agency. And Gypsy was strikingly beautiful *and* she was estranged from her family. It turned out her mother and two siblings sided with her stepfather, accusing her of falsely accusing him of rape. As a result, her molester still lived in the family home her late father had built.

The pimp's modus operandi was to purposefully get the girls hooked on heroin through a process of subtle manipulation. He knew once these girls were junkies they would do anything, sexual or otherwise, to score their next fix. Like others of his ilk, he'd discovered there was a point in heroin addiction that a junkie's biological needs would override any inhibitions, reservations or morals a girl may have.

The pimp would then *feed* these young women through to the agency, which then hired them out for an exorbitant hourly rate to well-heeled clients who included high flying businessmen, lawyers, accountants and other professionals, film industry people and the odd politician. The clients also included Heck Williams who, at that time, was still a year away from making deputy chief.

Williams became one of Gypsy's regular clients. He was also her most violent client and sometimes beat her. Reflecting on that, she realized he'd have beaten her more often had the agency not begun charging him for the time off she needed to recover from the cuts and bruises she'd sustained. Time the agency couldn't otherwise charge out.

Through sheer willpower and the discovery of an inner strength she never knew she had, along with the timely intervention of a neighborhood priest who had been alerted to the girl's plight, Gypsy had eventually conquered her drug addiction after the priest enrolled her in a rehab clinic for teens. She'd also quit the escort agency, reclaimed her real name and then, as Suzie Fox, had worked two jobs to not only finish high school, but also put herself thru UCLA.

Suzie's change of fortunes hadn't ended there. She'd graduated from the university with honors, and, after acquitting herself well as a member of the mayor's election canvassing team, had scored her plum career job with *Boutique PR*. In the process it was fair to say she'd gotten her life together.

That gave her no small sense of pride. Even so, the shame attached to her time as Gypsy Diamond hung over her like a black cloud. She could never quite escape its shadow.

Williams had continued to stalk her after she left the agency, but a change of address and an unlisted phone number had somehow put an end to his persistence.

Until now.

Now the bastard wants another piece of me.

6

Taking stock of her feelings, she realized it was only in the past couple of days she had pulled herself together and begun thinking straight. Until mid-week, she'd been in a zombie-like daze, operating on auto-pilot.

Her employer had suspected something was up. She recalled being summoned into his office on the Monday following her encounter with the crooked cop.

◀◀◀◀

I suspected I was for it when my manager's P.A. advised me the boss wanted to see me and he wanted to see me *now*. It was early afternoon. I'd spent most of the morning fighting to stay awake for the duration of Boutique PR's weekly staff meeting. Not because I was disinterested, but because I'd gotten little sleep over the weekend after my run-in with Williams. To say I was stressed to the eyeballs was no exaggeration.

"You wanted to see me, Bill?" I asked as I looked into the manager's office.

"Close the door and take a seat, Suzie," fifty-year-old Bill Swainson said.

I did as he directed.

"Is something wrong?" I asked.

"You tell me," the balding, snappily dressed manager said. "You haven't been your normal bubbly self today. And you were as quiet as a mouse at this morning's meeting."

I suddenly found the chair I was sitting on uncomfortable and I began fidgeting. I'd been trying to keep it all together at work, but I realized I'd failed miserably.

"Just a personal problem I'm trying to work through on the home front, Bill… I've been trying not to let it impact on my work…"

Swainson fastened his all-knowing eyes on me. He didn't miss much, and that only made me more nervous in his presence.

"Do you need some time off?" he asked.

I'd have loved some time off, but I felt that wouldn't be a good look for someone who had only just started at the firm.

"No, but thanks anyway. I'm…I'm sure I'll sort it out soon."

"Is there anything I can do?"

This was a side of Swainson I hadn't seen. He had a reputation as a manager who set high standards, who was only interested in the bottom line and who didn't suffer fools, but he was showing a compassionate side I hadn't noticed before.

Should I confide in him? God knows I could do with an ally right now.

"I don't think so, thanks Bill. But I'll let you know if anything changes."

"Good. Well make sure you do." Changing direction, he asked, "Now, are you all set for tomorrow?"

I knew he was referring to a new assignment that would see me working out of the offices of my new client *Chisholm Security* for the rest of the week. It was a familiarization exercise suggested by Swainson and readily agreed to by his opposite at the security firm, the goal being to fast-track my understanding of their operation.

"All set, yes."

"Good."

Swainson stood up, indicating the meeting was over.

"Well good luck, and don't forget... Let me know if you need help with anything."

Departing the office, I said, "Thanks Bill, I appreciate it."

As the cab continued its crawl toward the *Sheraton Grand*, Suzie felt increasingly nervous. Every spare minute these past few days had been spent preparing for what she was about to do. She'd exhaustively gone through every single aspect of her plan, leaving nothing to chance. It had involved long hours of study, rehearsals and one-woman roleplays until she was ready to scream.

Suzie checked her sequined shoulder bag for possibly the sixth time since leaving for the hotel. Amongst the cosmetics and other personal items in it was something she hoped would be her salvation. She then pulled a small mirror from her bag and examined her face. Her smoldering blue green eyes stared back at her.

I hope you know what you're doing, girlfriend.

7

Suzie adjusted her long, brown hair, which had been elegantly styled in the *updo* fashion courtesy of a visit to her hair stylist that morning, then returned the mirror to her bag.

Up front, the cabbie, a middle-aged veteran of the streets, cursed as the vehicle they followed braked suddenly. He honked the horn and leaned out the window to abuse the other driver.

"No idea!" the cabbie complained, more for his passenger's benefit than anyone else.

Again the traffic began moving.

Ignoring all outside distractions, Suzie went over her plans once more. What she was about to do would require guts and perfect timing. Just thinking about it made her feel sick to the stomach.

It's your only option if you want to protect the life you've created for yourself!

In an attempt to take her mind off what she had to do, she cast her mind back to the Tuesday just gone. It was the first day she had to work out of the offices of her client *Chisholm Security*.

◀◀◀◀

After being made to wait forty-five minutes in Chisholm Security's reception area, I found myself sitting opposite Ted Hornby, Chisholm's impressive, high achieving founder. The forty-three-year old former White House security advisor wasn't especially tall, but he had a hard look about him. He also possessed an IQ that was through the roof, knew everything there was to know about security and had all the attributes of a leader.

It's fair to say I felt slightly intimidated in his presence.

"Now, did Bill brief you on what's in store for you this week?" Hornby asked, fastening his clear, blue eyes on me.

"Only that I'll be observing all aspects of your operation, Mister Hornby. He said that I–"

I stopped talking when my client held his hand up.

"It's Ted," Hornby said, smiling for the first time. "And yes you'll observe every aspect of our operation… except those aspects that are commercially sensitive. How much do you know about us?"

I realized he was testing me.

"I know that Chisholm is a newcomer in the security field, but its personnel are the best of the best and its systems are cutting edge."

Hornby snapped his fingers triumphantly and pointed at me.

"You got it! And before the week's out you'll understand why we'll be number one in our field within the next five years here on the West Coast."

"If not the whole country," I suggested.

"Exactly," Hornby agreed. "And when you come up to speed you'll be the interface between Chisholm and the media."

"I'm looking forward to that, Ted."

"Good…We are putting a lot of trust in you, so don't let me down."

Hornby reached out and pushed an intercom button on his desktop before I could respond.

"Send Andy through will you?" he said when an unseen secretary answered. Looking back at me, he said, "I believe you've met Andy Davis."

"I believe so, yes," I confirmed.

I clearly recalled meeting Davis. The New Yorker was, after all, a good looking, intelligent and engaging individual albeit too brash for my tastes. I met him at an after-work meet-and-greet function hosted by my firm two weeks earlier. That had been my first official engagement at *Boutique PR* and I recalled I'd been very nervous.

8

Moments later, Davis entered the office. The twenty-seven-year-old New Yorker nodded to me as soon as he saw me, confirming that he, too, recalled our first meeting.

"You've met, Susan Fox I believe," Hornby said.

"Yes," Davis confirmed. Extending his hand to me, he said, "Hello again Susan."

"Hello," I said accepting the other's hand. "And it's Suzie."

Addressing me, Hornby said, "Andy's our systems manager, Susan... ah... Suzie. He'll be your chaperone and main point of contact over the next four days, so anything you need to know... he's the man."

I surreptitiously studied Davis. Even though he wasn't my type, I could well imagine some women would find him attractive. Certainly, my female colleagues considered him quite a catch. Tall with dark, flashing eyes and a ready smile, he looked self-assured and oozed total confidence.

Pity he's so damned brash.

Hornby then suggested Davis take me to his office and begin my education. We departed and over the next hour the systems manager explained what was in store for me over the coming days.

I quickly realized I had an exhaustive schedule and a big learning curve ahead of me, and I just hoped I'd be up to it. Especially with everything else that was going on in my life. I was already feeling exhausted and the day had hardly begun.

Just put on a brave face my girl and pretend everything is hunky dory.

My recent confrontation with Deputy Chief Williams was never far from mind. I tried not to think about it or about the coming Friday, which was D-Day – the day the deadline he reluctantly agreed to expired. I still didn't know what I was going to do about that.

Despite our busy schedule, Davis found time to hit on me. For my part, I wasn't any more attracted to him than I had been the first time I met him. I still considered him brash and was more convinced than ever we had little in common.

So it was with some misgivings I accepted an invitation to join him at a downtown bar for drinks after work.

"One drink," I said.

"One drink," Davis agreed. His confident expression signaled he didn't really believe that.

I had accepted the invitation despite an inner voice that told me I should avoid socializing with anyone let alone with members of the opposite sex until I'd resolved my current problem. That problem being Deputy Chief Williams.

As it turned out the drinks took my mind off my unenviable predicament, and I was pleasantly surprised by how personable my drinking companion could be.

It could be an act, I warned myself.

One drink led to two and could very well have resulted in my accepting an invitation to join my companion for dinner had my inner voice not spoken to me again. This time I listened.

Davis warned me he wouldn't give up. I told him I'd be surprised if he did.

9

By the time I returned to my cramped, two-bedroom apartment, the effects of the alcohol and pleasant company had worn off and reality had returned. There was only three days to go until I'd be hearing from Williams again and I was starting to panic.

After depositing my satchel on the dining table, I threw open the windows. The sound of rush hour traffic carried to the fifth floor, but it was soon drowned out by the beat of *The Black Eyed Peas* when I cranked their latest hit up full volume courtesy of my *Alexa* speakers.

I was thankful to have the apartment to myself. My fellow tenant, an *American Airlines* flight attendant, was away on one of her long haul flights, which suited me just fine. I didn't need any more distractions right now. I had planned to work out at my local gym before dinner, but my routines had been shot to hell since my encounter with my old nemesis and so I decided to settle for a light workout in an alcove adjoining my bedroom.

After guzzling some chilled water from the fridge, I changed into gym shorts and tee-shirt then began performing a quick routine I'd devised – a combination of light aerobics and yoga – to compensate for the canceled gym workout.

Unfortunately, my mind was elsewhere so I flagged it before I'd even raised a sweat then showered and changed before using a food app on my phone to order a Chinese to go. When the meal finally arrived, I realized I had no appetite and so consigned the food to the fridge.

This day is going from bad to worse.

I debated whether to go out. My girlfriends had mentioned they'd be meeting up at one of our favorite downtown watering holes tonight, but I realized I couldn't face them. Not tonight. And so I settled for an early night.

That turned out to be a bad idea. I slept poorly and what little sleep I was able to snatch was punctuated with dreams of incidents I'd rather forget. Williams and my stepfather were both to the fore in some of those dreams.

I finally fell into a deep sleep just before dawn and slept until mid-morning, sleeping through the alarm and through two incoming phone calls. Upon waking I would discover one call was from my employer and the other from my client, both wondering where the hell I was.

When I surfaced, I realized I couldn't face work. I felt as if I hadn't slept a wink, but worse, Williams' threat to expose my past had left me feeling stressed to the eyeballs and depressed. Worse still, I felt powerless – just as I had when my stepfather was abusing me.

I could tell my mental state was worsening by the day.

The same questions kept coming to me.

Did I ask for this? Is this what I deserve?

I was starting to wonder if this was my karma.

Is this somehow my fault?

There was no doubt people were starting to notice the change in me and it was impacting on my work bigtime.

Dragging myself from bed, I phoned my manager's P.A. at *Boutique PR* and advised her I had contracted the flu and would likely need the remainder of the week to recover. I hated having to do that. Especially as I'd only recently started the new job and was already being questioned about the quality of my work. It was the first time I'd ever pulled a sickie and I swore it would be the last. Thankfully, the P.A. volunteered to phone my client at *Chisholm Security* on my behalf.

I thought about breakfast, but couldn't face it so went back to bed feeling sorry for myself. I found myself crying a lot. My moods swung between depression and anger. I was depressed my past had caught up with me and angry I couldn't fight back. Suicidal feelings I hadn't experienced since my mid-teens suddenly threatened to overwhelm me.

Heck Williams has me where he wants me and he knows it!

10

Lying in bed, I had plenty of time to think. By lunchtime, I decided it was time to do something to resolve my predicament.

But what? I can't go to the authorities.

I didn't know where to turn or what to do. I had a wide network of friends, male friends included, but none so close I felt I could confide in. Not about the predicament I'd found herself in. Very few of them knew about my past life and I wanted it to stay that way. I knew if I revealed how Williams was blackmailing me, it would all come out.

As for reporting him to the authorities that remains out of the question given what he has on me. Besides, everyone knows the LAPD always protect their own.

A rumbling tummy told me I had to eat. I hadn't eaten since the previous lunchtime and so I dressed and then hurried through to the kitchen. Retrieving the Chinese food from the fridge, I microwaved it and sat down to eat it at the kitchen table.

My eyes were drawn to my laptop, which sat unopened on the tabletop nearby.

An old saying suddenly came to me.

"Know your enemy," I murmured, paraphrasing the famous Sun Tzu proverb. It was one my late father often quoted although I never could remember who it was exactly he was quoting. I thought it might have been Douglas MacArthur.

Booting up my laptop, I Googled "Deputy Chief Hector Williams, LAPD" online.

Exactly what I hoped to achieve I wasn't sure. All I knew was I still had my reputation and I was determined to protect that regardless of the cost.

Within half an hour of surfing the net, a picture had begun to emerge. Williams was a career cop who had a reputation for dealing harshly with offenders. Reportedly, he'd been the subject of internal disciplinary action within the department on several occasions.

Reading between the lines, it was clear Williams' tough policing methods coincided with a more hard-nosed attitude toward law enforcement in Los Angeles by the city fathers, lawmakers and politicians. They wanted their law enforcers to start kicking ass and they made no secret of it.

I studied a press photo of Williams on the screen. Taken three years earlier, it showed a then forty-six-year-old Williams at the official presentation commemorating his promotion to the rank of deputy chief at the LAPD. He was smiling, but I could see his eyes remained as cold as ever. I shivered involuntarily and clicked on another site.

A recent press release popped up showing a photo of Williams with his attractive wife Pamela and their two teenage sons taken at a Rotarians' family dinner. The caption stated that the deputy chief was vice-president of the Westside Rotary Club. It also reminded readers that

Pamela Williams was the oldest daughter of the current Governor of California.

So, you married above your station, Hector.

11

I was starting to understand that Williams was considered a pillar of the community. I also wondered if Missus Williams knew of her husband's extracurricular activities, or if anyone else did for that matter.

Before ending my search, I happened upon a report that connected Williams with the mayoral function scheduled for the *Sheraton Grand Hotel* this coming Friday – the same function I was planning to attend. It appeared the deputy chief would be one of several senior LAPD officers at the function.

"Nearly there," the cabbie said, interrupting his fare's thoughts.

Suzie looked up and saw the upper floors of the *Sheraton Grand* above the tops of the vehicles ahead.

This would be her second visit to the plush hotel in as many days. She had visited its conference room the previous afternoon, officially to check out the function venue in her capacity as a former member of the mayor's team of canvassers, but unofficially to hide something in the ladies' restroom.

She was aware the hidden item would have been detected had she tried to smuggle it into the hotel today. Security staff with their metal detectors would most certainly have found it as they checked each guest upon arrival. Once inside the hotel, she didn't envisage any problem retrieving the item from the restroom.

Suzie could feel her heart rate rising as the cab pulled into the hotel arrivals area and stopped outside the front entrance.

A hotel valet hurried to open Suzie's door as she paid the cabbie.

The cabbie watched admiringly as the young woman walked off. She was his most beautiful fare of the day. No doubt about it.

Ignoring the impatience of another cabbie who had pulled up behind him, he watched as his passenger walked assuredly through the entrance. She looked a knockout in her black, figure-hugging, cocktail dress and high heels. The courageous young woman displayed no signs of the nerves that were assailing her at that moment.

Suzie entered the ladies' restroom adjoining the hotel's conference room. She saw at a glance one of the cubicles was in use, and, as luck would have it, it was the very cubicle in which she'd hidden the item she'd come to retrieve. She filled in time touching up her lipstick and adjusting her hair in the wall mirror.

Two other guests visited the restroom before the woman using the cubicle of most interest to Suzie finally emerged. A middle-aged spinster-type with blue-rinsed hair and a permanently gloomy countenance, she took her time washing and drying her hands before leaving, scarcely giving the younger woman a second glance.

Suzie entered the cubicle, reached around behind the toilet cistern and retrieved the item she'd hidden there the previous afternoon. Placing it in her shoulder bag, she left the restroom, and, hiding her apprehension behind a smile, walked through to mingle with the other guests in the conference room.

The hum of conversation in the large room was almost deafening and all but drowned out Bizet's *Carmen*, which was being played by a string quartet hired for the occasion. Laughter rang out as guests caught up with friends and sampled the champagne and other beverages on offer.

Somewhere nearby, one of hundreds of balloons in the room popped with a loud *BANG!* causing Suzie and more than a few others to jump. This only served to prompt more laughter.

Suzie stopped to exchange pleasantries with mayoral staffers, elected councilors and fellow volunteers she'd met while canvassing for Mayor Lopez. As she circulated, she was very aware she was attracting admiring glances. Her high heels gave her extra height, which meant she didn't have to look up to too many of the men in the room.

Invited media personnel caught her eye and she was pleased to see they were here in numbers. They would serve her purpose nicely this evening. She identified reporters from the *Los Angeles Times*, *CNN News*, *KNX Radio*, *USA Today*, *Fox News* and even *The Washington Post*, and she noticed press photographers and TV cameramen among them. As usual at such occasions, the media reps congregated close to the bar, partaking of the free booze. More than a few of them seemed to have already had a drink or two, too many.

Please stay sober tonight boys and girls. You'll have some breaking news to cover soon.

12

The media presence reminded Suzie of an interesting meeting she had two days earlier with a contact at the *Los Angeles Times*. That meeting had been catalyst for what she was planning to do in the next few minutes.

As soon as I finished researching Hector Williams online I phoned Mel Harper, a former UCLA classmate who happened to be a court reporter at the *Los Angeles Times*. It had been some time since we'd spoken. I just hoped she remembered me.

"Mel, it's Suzie Fox," I said when she answered the phone.

"Suzie? Hi! What's up?"

"Whew, that's a relief. I wasn't sure you'd remember me."

"You're joking, right? I'm not likely to forget the most beautiful high achiever in UCLA's Class of twenty eighteen."

"Well, thanks for the compliment, but I'm not sure it's deserved... Anyway, Mel, I was hoping you could help me."

"Sure. Shoot, but make it quick…I'm on deadline."

I quickly explained I wanted background information on Deputy Chief Williams. To sweeten the pot, I added that it may result in a major news story developing. Mel said she'd dig up what she could and suggested we meet somewhere in a couple of hours when her shift finished. I asked her to name the place and she suggested Grand Park as that was on her way home.

Two hours later, I found myself sharing one of Grand Park's famous pink benches with my old UCLA classmate. Talking to her now, it felt as though we were old friends yet we'd never been close at university. I now couldn't help wondering why that was the case. We seemed to click straight away.

The bench we shared was shaded by a flowering camellia tree and it overlooked the park's water fountain. All around, people young and old, visitors and residents alike, enjoyed the many attractions the iconic park offered.

Mel and I slurped on ice-creams I'd purchased at a nearby kiosk.

"So, I dug around in the Times' archives and sneaked a peak at one or two of my colleagues' unpublished notes as well," Mel said. "I turned up some interesting stuff on your Deputy Chief Williams."

"Oh?"

"Yeah, he has quite a reputation for using roughhouse tactics it seems and has been subjected to internal disciplinary measures on more than a few occasions."

"That tallies with my research."

"Seems he was fast-tracked to Deputy Chief of Police status despite his reputation… or maybe *because of* his reputation."

"*Because* I suspect… Maybe his approach to the job suited the LAPD's new no-nonsense approach to crime."

"That and a suspicion that his father-in-law, the Governor, leaned on the police department's hierarchy… That's what my newsroom colleagues say anyway."

"Interesting."

I pondered that for a moment.

Mel asked, "What's your interest in the deputy chief anyway?"

I looked at the young court reporter. As well as having a sharp, inquiring mind, she was someone I felt was on the same wavelength as myself. In that moment I had an overwhelming desire to share with her the burden I'd been carrying these past few days.

"This is strictly off the record, right?" I said.

"Of course," Mel said.

I took a deep breath and told her everything that had happened to me since coming to California. I left nothing out. Not even my former drug-taking or escort agency escapades. The only things I withheld were the childhood experiences that prompted me to stray from the straight and narrow in the first place.

Mel was momentarily speechless.

"My God!" she said. "I would never have picked it…You seemed so…so together when I knew you at UCLA. So…innocent in a way."

"Well, you know what they say…Never judge a book by its cover."

"How are you coping with all this now then?"

"Well, that's the thing," I confided. "I'm not. At all."

Before I knew it I was crying.

Mel placed a caring arm around me and held me. It felt good to be able to share my problems with another caring soul.

"You can't go to someone at the LAPD?" she asked.

I shook my head.

"It would only be my word against his. Anyway, the LAPD–"

"I know," Mel said, interjecting. "The LAPD always protect their own."

We sat in companionable silence for a few minutes, watching young children who were squealing with delight as they frolicked in the shallow waters of the fountain.

At length, Mel said, "It's a pity you didn't get him on tape."

I looked at her and suddenly smiled. She didn't know it, but she'd just given me an idea.

We parted with the promise we'd catch up soon. It was a promise I intended to keep. I sensed Mel could be a true friend.

13

Later that afternoon, I phoned Andy Davis at *Chisholm Security*.

"Suzie, how are you?" he asked. "I heard you came down with the flu."

To my ears it didn't sound like he believed for one second I had the flu and my response to his comment sounded even less convincing.

With that out of the way, I said, "Andy, I need to secretly record someone to get them off my back."

Davis said nothing for a moment.

At length he said, "Record them…Like get them on tape you mean?"

"Yes."

"Why not record *and* film them?"

"Is that possible?"

"Anything's possible," the cocky New Yorker said. "Who is the target anyway?"

"I…I'm afraid I can't say."

"Well, we have a problem then. Our company policy dictates we don't provide film or audio devices for clandestine use unless we know who the unsuspecting target is, and even then it's left to our discretion as to whether we assist."

I could tell he was quoting by heart from Chisholm's policy manual.

Time for a little white lie I think.

"Sonny Matthews is his name…He's an ex boyfriend who is trying to blackmail me for money."

Davis immediately sympathized with my plight and asked if he could sort my ex out for me. I assured him I preferred to go with my plan so he recommended a device called *Argus X25*.

"It's a new, cutting-edge, mini-spy camera with audio capability and it can be attached to your person or to a handbag or suchlike."

"Sounds expensive."

"It is…*if* you buy it. You can rent it from us on a day-to-day basis if you prefer."

I liked the sound of that. We quickly negotiated a very reasonable price, which I suspect he handsomely discounted, and I arranged for it to be couriered to me overnight.

Before I could sign off, Davis said, "About that dinner engagement…"

"What dinner engagement?"

"The one I'm about to ask you about."

We both laughed.

"You don't give up, do you?" I said.

"I told you I wouldn't."

I could picture him smiling.

"Look Andy, let me get this little problem I'm working on out of the way and we can revisit this, okay?"

He accepted that with good grace and we agreed to talk about it later. Whether I'd ever take him up on his offer I wasn't sure.

Suzie realized Mayor Lopez was smiling her way. She returned the smile as Lopez and his pretty wife Maria continued to work the hotel's crowded conference room.

The young account exec scooped a glass of champagne from the tray of a waiter as he walked past. She took one sip and then froze when she saw Heck Williams standing head and shoulders above almost everyone else in the room. The deputy chief was with five other senior LAPD officers. Senior amongst them was Chief of Police Paul Henderson, a heavy set, older man, who appeared to be doing most of the talking.

14

Seeing Williams reminded her of her encounter with her nemesis outside LAPD headquarters that morning when she'd basically ambushed him as he arrived for work.

Early on the Friday morning I caught a cab to LAPD headquarters to await the arrival of Deputy Chief Williams at the start of his working day. An earlier phone call to his office confirmed he was expected. Exactly when he'd turn up and which entrance he'd use was anyone's guess. I was gambling he'd use the main entrance and I hoped he wasn't planning a late start. However, I was resigned to a long wait. I glanced at my watch. It was only seven thirty.

I chose to wait on a wooden bench on the sidewalk diagonally opposite the main entrance. It provided an unobstructed view of everyone coming and going.

Whilst waiting, I mentally rehearsed what I was going to say to Williams. I was mindful it wouldn't be an easy conversation. I needed him to confirm for the record he was blackmailing me for sex or otherwise say something incriminating and hope that the spy camera I'd been fitted with captured everything.

The device had arrived the previous morning by overnight courier courtesy of Andy Davis. The so-called simple instructions to fit and activate it had proven anything but simple, and I'd had to phone Davis twice to talk me through it. On the second call, he'd referred me to one of his firm's junior techies who, after another two protracted phone calls, had agreed to call into my apartment to personally activate the device.

Five minutes was all it had taken to activate the spy camera and fit it to the pocket of a casual shirt I planned to wear. The device itself was smaller in diameter than a dollar coin and totally innocuous.

Whilst awaiting the arrival of my target, I had to consciously restrain myself from touching or fidgeting with the miniature camera still attached to my shirt pocket. The techie had warned that messing with it could cause a malfunction in the camera's film or audio function, or possibly both, and I didn't want that.

Williams arrived at eight sharp. Just as well, too, as I'd have had to find a restroom if he'd left it much later.

Crossing the street, I timed it so that I intercepted the deputy chief in between two pillars a little distance from the entrance to LAPD HQ. The pillars concealed us from the security cameras that lined the near side of the building – something I suspected Williams would be very aware of and would be thankful for.

"Deputy Chief Williams," I said, standing in front of the big cop.

Williams couldn't hide his surprise. His first instinct was to scan for the security cameras. I couldn't be certain, but I thought I saw relief in his eyes when he realized we were concealed from them.

You can't hide from my camera though, Hector.

I looked into his eyes and I saw the cold, hard stare of my nightmares once again.

15

"What the hell are you doing here?" Williams asked.

"I wanted to let you know my decision," I said.

Williams looked around nervously. Given our close proximity to his workplace and the fact I had ambushed him, he was instantly suspicious.

Knowing that cops, or veteran cops like him at least, were wise to the ways of the streets and the people whose paths they crossed, I was afraid he would see right through my act. Worse, I feared he might search me and discover I was trying to set him up. Drawing on my previous experience on the streets as a working girl, I portrayed via subtle facial expressions that I was coming to him in a submissive state.

Williams remained on high alert. Unsure how to react, he looked at me then glanced around yet again. Finally, his inner urges overrode his policeman's instincts. He grabbed me by the arm and led me around the corner so that we were further removed from the security cameras.

"You could've phoned me," he said, still trying to gauge my

intentions. "So why did you come here?"

He looked into my eyes as if searching for any deception hidden there.

"I wanted to see you personally, Hector…and also to make a counter offer."

Negotiating like this was all part of my pre-planned spiel. I had predicted that if I'd just agreed to his original terms, he might smell a rat. I was aware I needed to make this convincing so it reflected my personality and matched the intelligence expected of a UCLA honors graduate.

He's sure to know I'm an honors grad. He knows everything else about me!

"A counter offer?" Williams almost spat the words out. "You don't have a leg to stand on, you little bitch."

"I realize that, Hector. That's why I'm here. If there was any way out of this, I wouldn't be here now, would I? I'd be telling you to fuck off instead of working out a deal for you to fuck me, right?"

Williams nodded and his lip curled into a smile. He seemed to be enjoying that I had attitude and that I openly despised him yet was agreeing to sleep with him anyway.

I continued, "So, after thinking about my life…and your threat to inform my employer about my past indiscretions if I don't sleep with you, I agree to have sex with you Deputy Chief Williams, but only for two weeks. No more."

Williams stifled a laugh when he saw I wasn't joking.

"And why would I agree to two weeks, whore?"

"Because two weeks as your sex slave is the maximum I can endure.

Any longer and I'd rather give in to your blackmail and risk losing the life and career I've earned here in L.A."

Williams seemed predictably pissed that I was daring to negotiate with him. Yet behind his anger I sensed he was turned on by the thought he was forcing me into sexual submission once more.

I set my jaw and stared at him.

"Two weeks and that's it."

I held out my hand.

"Will you shake on that, Hector?"

Of course I knew he wouldn't honor any such agreement even if he shook on it, but I had to give the impression I believed he would and that I had formulated a plan that would get him off my back when the fortnight was up.

The bastard thought long and hard before finally shaking my hand.

"I have a mayoral function after work, so you'll see me around nine tonight," he said. As he walked away, he added, "Be naked and alone in your apartment, bitch, or there'll be consequences!"

I turned and walked off in the opposite direction. I hope he didn't notice, but I had a spring in my step. I was also grinning to myself like a Cheshire cat.

Looking at Williams and the other police officers, Suzie took a deep breath as she steeled herself to do what she'd come to do. She was painfully aware the next few minutes would determine whether she'd continue her promising career as a public relations exec or whether she'd spend the foreseeable future behind bars.

It's now or never.

16

The same waiter who passed by moments earlier walked past again, and Suzie placed her near-full champagne glass on the now empty tray he carried. Keeping her eye on Williams, she began weaving her way through the crowd. As she did, she tried to stay calm. It wasn't easy. She was breathing so hard she feared she might hyperventilate, and she was starting to perspire even though it was a cool evening by Californian standards.

Suzie glanced down to confirm the shoulder bag she carried was open. She reached into it with her left hand and felt around for the item she'd retrieved from the ladies' restroom. Its cold, metallic touch gave her some comfort.

Nearing the LAPD officers, she was relieved to see they remained preoccupied, laughing at a joke Chief Henderson was telling. None of them noticed her sidle up to them.

As she prepared to act, a feeling of nausea rose up in her throat. She could feel her heart hammering in her chest and she was starting to shake noticeably. Worse, she could feel what little courage was left draining away and she suddenly feared she couldn't complete what she'd set out to do.

Get your shit together, girl!

One by one, the police officers became aware they were being scrutinized by the beautiful young woman who was now only a few feet away.

Suzie found herself looking up into Williams' cold, gray eyes. In that moment she saw recognition and then confusion flash in those same eyes.

Faking a dazzling, Hollywood-esque smile, Suzie walked up to Williams, her right hand extended as if she was greeting an old friend. Her left hand remained inside her shoulder bag.

"Good evening, Deputy Chief Williams," she said, confidently grasping the man's right hand in hers. Her heart was beating so hard now she feared it might explode.

A bemused Williams reciprocated, shaking Suzie's hand with a grimace that might have passed for a smile.

17

In a move Suzie had rehearsed so many times she could execute it in her sleep, she pulled a set of steel handcuffs from her bag whilst retaining her grip on Williams' hand. She deftly cuffed the deputy chief's right wrist then released her hold on his hand and cuffed her own right wrist, effectively shackling herself to him.

An audible *CLICK!* signaled to all the police officers and indeed to anyone familiar with the sound that the unlikely couple were now shackled to each other and would remain that way until someone unlocked the handcuffs. The entire process took two-and-a-half seconds.

"What the…?" a shocked Williams asked.

The astonished cop tried to pull away from Suzie, but she was staying with him whether he wanted her company or not. His eyes flashed surprise, anger, confusion and embarrassment all at once.

Speaking in a loud, clear voice, Suzie said, "Deputy Chief Hector Williams of the Los Angeles Police Department, I, Susan Fox, an American woman, hereby make a citizen's arrest."

Williams and his fellow officers appeared stunned. This was something new for all of them, and none of them remotely knew how they were meant to react.

Suzie was pleased to see she now had the attention of everyone in the room. You could hear a proverbial pin drop.

Looking up at Williams and reciting the lines she'd rehearsed countless times, she continued, "I arrest you for crimes, which include blackmail, extortion and threatened rape."

Suzie wasn't certain *threatened rape* was actually an official legal term, but she thought it important to include in her prepared speech. It was true after all.

In an even more surreal moment, she began reciting the *Miranda warning* to Williams.

"You have the right to remain silent," she said. "Anything you say can be used against you in court…"

She momentarily petered out as she forgot the rest of the official arrest warning.

Looking pointedly at the deputy chief's colleagues, she added, "I ask that you cooperate with me until police take you into custody."

Only now did Williams react.

"This is ridiculous!" he shouted so everyone could hear. "I am a proud officer of the law and have never blackmailed or threatened to rape anyone!"

18

Suzie glanced at the other guests and was delighted to see the media representatives were starting to swarm around like vultures. Two of the newspaper photographers were already snapping photos, a *Fox News* cameraman armed with a shoulder-mounted camera was already filming the unfolding drama and behind him a *CNN News* cameraman was positioning himself to begin filming.

The beautiful young woman who was now the attention of everyone in the room, reached into her bag with her free hand and pulled out a small package, which she held above her head.

Williams pulled Suzie close to his chest and murmured, "What the hell do you think you're doing?"

He was so close Suzie could smell his breath. His eyes bored into hers, and she saw the malice in them.

Finding courage she didn't know she had, she calmly whispered, "Sending you to where you belong, Heck. That's what I'm doing."

She looked back at the package she was holding and, in a loud voice, continued addressing the assembled.

"This contains film and audio of Deputy Chief Williams recorded just this morning. Film and audio which conclusively prove my accusations of blackmail, extortion and threatened rape are all true."

A shocked silence prevailed as the assembled digested the bombshell Suzie had just dropped. And then pandemonium broke out.

An ashen-faced Williams began cursing and protesting his innocence; his fellow LAPD officers came to his support, insisting there must be some mistake; the reporters began firing questions at Williams and at Suzie; and the other guests began shouting and talking all at once.

Lightbulbs flashed as press photographers shot some of the most newsworthy photos they were ever likely to shoot, and excited reporters spoke into their mics or scribbled on their shorthand pads as they covered what for most must surely be the most newsworthy event of the year if not the decade.

19

"**W**ho is the victim of these alleged crimes, Miss Fox?" the female *Los Angeles Times* reporter yelled at Suzie. "Is it you? Is it you he threatened to rape?"

The reporter had to shout at the top of her lungs to make herself heard above the commotion.

"What do you say to the charges, Deputy Chief Williams?" the *New York Times* reporter yelled at Williams.

Above the din, Chief Henderson called for calm.

"Quiet!" the chief yelled a second time. As the noise settled, he turned to Suzie. "Miss Fox, I'm sure there must be some mistake," he said.

"There's no mistake!" Suzie snapped. "The camera doesn't lie, and neither do I –"

"I'm sure you –"

"I'd remind you I have film and audio of Deputy Chief Williams, which incriminate him in the crimes I have him accused of," she insisted, speaking right over top of the LAPD chief. Still addressing

Henderson, she looked at Williams and added, "I have him cold."

Williams looked balefully at her. There was murder in his eyes.

"I'm sure you *think* you have evidence of some sort," Henderson said smoothly, "but let's go back to my office and see if we can get to the bottom of this. We have procedures that –"

"One minute, Chief Henderson!"

It was a man's voice. An authoritative voice.

Henderson looked around to see Mayor Lopez pushing his way toward him through the crowd.

Lopez, a distinguished defense lawyer in his past life, had been observing the unfolding drama with interest – as had everyone else.

Standing before Henderson, Lopez said, "Correct me if I'm wrong Chief, but any American citizen has the right to make a formal citizen's arrest if they believe they have just cause."

The re-elected mayor glared at the chief as if challenging him to disagree.

"Well, yes Mayor Lopez, but –"

"But nothing, Chief!" the mayor said. "I know Miss Fox personally and can attest to her good character. She is an honest, law abiding citizen and if she thinks she has just cause" – he looked at Suzie – "as she obviously does, then you shouldn't need to be told she's within her rights…and you, as a senior officer of the law, are obliged to take the accused into custody for questioning."

"Ah, yes…of course you are right, Mayor Lopez," Henderson stammered as the television news cameramen and newspaper photographers pushed forward and camera flashbulbs lit up the room.

Turning to his fellow officers, or those of them who weren't under arrest at least, the chief pointed at Williams and said, "Read Deputy Chief Williams his rights and take him straight to my office at HQ."

20

Suzie tried not to show her delight at the way events were unfolding. She'd successfully manacled Williams and had made a citizen's arrest the police had to uphold. Mayor Lopez's unexpected support had been the icing on the cake.

The youngest of the police officers present asked Suzie for the package she was holding.

She handed it to him.

"Please don't lose it."

The officer smiled, embarrassed.

"Do you have the key to the handcuffs?" he asked.

"Sure."

Suzie retrieved the key from a side pocket in her shoulder bag and handed it to the officer. He fumbled as he tried to unlock the cuffs. Meanwhile, the photographers kept shooting, the TV cameramen continued filming, the reporters kept asking unanswered questions and Williams continued protesting his innocence.

Finally, the cuffs clicked open and Suzie was free of the man she'd come to consider the devil incarnate. She proudly looked on as the young officer read Williams his rights before he and another officer led the deputy chief away.

Although no longer manacled, the accused was clearly in police custody: the younger officer had one hand on Williams' left shoulder while the other officer had one hand on his right shoulder. To reach the exit, the trio had to push their way through a media scrum that had formed around them.

Henderson and the remaining officers looked ready to leave as well. In fact, the harried chief appeared downright anxious to leave.

Grim-faced, he looked at Suzie.

"You should accompany us to headquarters, Miss Fox. We'll have some questions for you."

Suzie nodded. Henderson's tone and stony expression told her loud and clear it was an invitation she couldn't refuse. Nevertheless, she was happy to oblige. She'd known all along it was very likely she'd be taken away for questioning.

The chief and the other two officers escorted Suzie from the conference room. As they departed, they ignored the questions reporters fired at them.

Suzie tried to remain composed in the middle of the media scrum that had formed. She was pleased everything was going to plan, but she knew it wasn't over.

Now comes the hard part. I have to make the charges stick.

21

The drive to LAPD HQ passed in silence inside the vehicle Suzie traveled in. No-one spoke and the tension was palpable.

Chief Henderson sat in the front passenger seat, staring straight ahead.

Suzie, who shared the rear seat with one of her escorts, found herself looking at the back of the chief's head, trying to work out what was going on inside it.

Upon arrival at HQ, Henderson ordered his subordinates to escort Suzie to a fourth floor meeting room and make her comfortable there (his words) while he went to his office.

Suzie guessed he was going to question his deputy first about the accusations she'd leveled at him.

How I'd love to be a fly on the wall.

Henderson rode alone in an elevator to his top floor office. Stepping out onto his floor, he received a call on his cellphone.

"Dammit!" he cursed when he saw who was calling.

Answering the call, he said, "Hello, Art."

"Are you on top of this clusterfuck, Paul?" Art Barrett asked.

Henderson sighed. Barrett was the serving City Council president and, as such, he was never slow to ride the LAPD if he thought the department wasn't performing. A migraine had prevented him from attending the mayoral function, but he'd evidently caught up on the evening's big news.

"You obviously heard about what went down tonight," the chief said.

"Heard about it? It's all over the airwaves for Chrissake!"

"Art, we–"

Barrett talked right over Henderson.

"Paul, your department can't afford any more bad press."

Henderson found himself nodding. He knew only too well what the president was referring to. The year had been a disaster for the LAPD from a public relations perspective.

Barrett continued, "Here's what you're gonna do…Discredit the woman and make this godawful problem go away."

"Go away?"

"How you do that is over to you…Keep me informed."

"I think it's too late for that, Art. I…"

Henderson stopped talking when he realized the president had ended the call.

22

Deep in thought, the chief strode to his office and entered it to find his deputy waiting for him with the same two officers who escorted him from the hotel. All three were sitting down and all three jumped to attention when they saw their superior.

"Sit down," Henderson said as he sat behind his desk.

The chief saw Williams' escorts had carried out his instructions and set up a video player on the desktop. He stared coldly at his deputy.

Fidgeting, Williams asked, "Am I officially under arrest, Chief?"

Henderson reached out and turned on a recording device on his desktop.

When he was satisfied it was recording, he said, "Whether or not you're officially under arrest Deputy Chief Williams depends on whether you can convince us of your innocence."

He then nodded to one of the other officers to start playing the film and accompanying audio Suzie had supplied.

#

In the meeting room she'd been deposited in, Suzie made herself as comfortable as she could on a couch in one corner of the room. It was going on for seven o'clock and she'd yet to be seen or questioned by anyone. Worse than that, she was stressed, hungry and tired.

The door opened and a young, female policewoman looked in.

"Can I get you a coffee, Miss Fox?" she asked.

"Coffee would be good, thanks," Suzie smiled. "Strong, black and no sugar."

Before the young cop could leave, Suzie asked, "Do you know how long I'm likely to be here?"

The policewoman shook her head.

"I'm sorry I don't."

The door closed on Suzie, leaving her alone once again.

23

In a French restaurant in Downtown L.A's Fashion District, Davis enjoyed an after-dinner drink alone at the bar. It was the same restaurant he'd had in mind when he recently invited Suzie to join him for a dinner date. So it was no coincidence he was thinking of her at that moment.

The beautiful account exec had been occupying his thoughts a lot of late. In the time he'd known her, albeit in a professional capacity, she had gotten under his skin. He found himself thinking about her all the time, and it bugged the hell out of him that she wasn't showing the same interest in him as he was in her. That was a new experience for the New Yorker. And that made him want her all the more.

Davis's attention was drawn to a television set behind the bar. It was tuned in to the *CNN News* channel, and a newsflash had just caught his eye.

Turning to the barman, he said, "Can you turn that up, bud?"

"Yup," the barman said, turning up the volume.

The young systems manager nearly choked on the cognac he was drinking when footage of Suzie handcuffed to Deputy Chief Williams appeared on screen. The footage began at the point where the beautiful young woman was holding the package above her head and advising her audience what it contained.

Davis immediately realized what Suzie wanted the spy camera for.

Within a minute, everyone in the bar was crowding around the TV set, spellbound.

The footage ended with Suzie being escorted from the hotel conference room in the company of two police officers.

A female *CNN News* presenter appeared on screen. She advised her audience the police officer under arrest and the courageous young woman responsible for his detainment had been taken to LAPD headquarters for questioning.

More recent footage screened, showing first Williams and then Suzie arriving under escort at the police department's HQ.

As the report ended, spontaneous cheering and applause erupted in the bar. None of the patrons or staffers had witnessed anything like they'd just seen.

Davis hardly noticed the others' reactions. The lone diner was already out the door before the report ended. He headed straight for his vehicle, a brand new, midnight blue *Mercedes-Benz* he'd purchased to impress the young woman he'd just seen on TV.

24

Suzie sensed she wouldn't be returning to her apartment any time soon. It was going on for eleven o'clock, Henderson and others had been grilling her for almost two hours and still there was no end in sight. The interviews had been exhausting and she was struggling to stay awake.

The young woman sensed her interrogators considered her *the enemy*. They made her feel as if she was the guilty party.

Guilty till proven innocent.

Tired beyond belief, she forced herself to listen to a question the chief was currently putting to her.

"And you refuse to say who provided the spy camera?" Henderson said, glaring at Suzie.

"For the moment, yes. I don't consider it important who actually helped me secure the evidence I supplied."

"You don't?"

"Nope."

"And you don't consider it important to reveal what information my deputy had on you that would constitute blackmail?"

Suzie was too tired to answer. She just shook her head.

"I'd remind you this interview is being recorded," Henderson said.

"*No*, I don't consider that important either."

You mentioned the recording you supplied was a copy.

"Yes."

"How many copies are there?"

Suzie was ready for this question. She knew the police would be anxious to get their hands on any and all copies of the incriminating recording – and not necessarily for any reasons that might aid her cause.

"More than one."

Henderson's eyes narrowed.

"How many more?"

"Two or three."

The chief was nearing the limit of his patience.

"Which is it?" he hissed. "Two or three?"

Suzie shrugged as if she didn't care.

"Maybe three…I don't remember exactly."

Henderson consciously restrained himself from reaching out and shaking the young woman.

"And where are these copies?"

"They are in safe hands," Suzie said, returning the other's cold stare.

A disgruntled Henderson switched the recorder off and headed for the still open door.

"Am I free to go?" Suzie asked.

"No you're not."

25

Minutes later, as he strode along the top floor corridor toward his office, Henderson received a call on his cellphone. *Caller ID* indicated it was council president Barrett calling. It was the third time he'd called since his first call earlier. The harried chief turned his phone off. He couldn't handle Barrett right now. Not with everything else that was going on.

In his office, Henderson looked at Williams and then at the two officers keeping the accused company. He wanted to try to wrap this up quickly, but he had a gut feeling this wasn't going to be an easy fix.

Addressing Williams, the chief asked, "What do you have to say for yourself, Heck?"

"As I already said, I'm totally innocent of the charges, Chief," a stressed Williams said.

"Well, the recording doesn't support that, does it?"

"The recording doesn't reveal my motives…I knew her when she was a junkie and a whore, and I was employing some tough love."

"Tough love?"

"Yessir. Once a heroin junkie always a junkie. That's my firm belief. And I was only trying to scare her into not getting back into that lifestyle…That is if she's not already using heroin again."

Henderson studied his deputy for a moment.

Changing tack, he said, "She *is* a beautiful woman, Heck, isn't she?"

Sensing he was being walked into a trap, Williams hesitantly agreed with his superior.

"Any blue-blooded man would want a piece of her, right?" the chief smiled.

"I guess," said Williams. He quickly added, "But I'd never force any woman to sleep with me if she didn't want to…Besides, I'm happily married. You know that."

His tone was almost pleading.

The chief looked at the other two officers. Their expressions remained neutral, but he could tell they didn't believe Williams any more than he did.

Turning back to his deputy, Henderson said, "That's one hell of a stretch, Heck. How do you think that's going to play out in a court of law?"

Williams said nothing for a few moments.

Finally, he said, "I want my lawyer."

"Of course you do."

Henderson considered his options.

Looking at the other two officers, he said, "You two, outside."

As the officers left the office, the chief stood up and followed them. On the way out, he glanced at Williams.

"And you...don't touch anything."

Closing the door behind him, he addressed the two officers who were now waiting close by in the corridor.

"I intend to stand Deputy Chief Williams down and release him on cognizance pending further investigation. You" – he looked at the younger of the two officers – "can finish processing the deputy chief now and then release him. And you" – he looked at the older of the two – "can prepare a report to give to the District Attorney first thing in the morning. Run it past me tonight before you sign off on it."

"Yes, Chief," the two officers said in unison.

Neither looked overjoyed. They knew they had a late night ahead of them – as did Henderson.

"The D.A. can decide whether Deputy Chief Williams has a case to answer to," the chief said. "Any questions?"

26

Alone inside the chief's office, Williams was trying to get his head around the fact Suzie had so dramatically turned the tables on him. He still couldn't believe the young woman was capable of what she'd achieved. A few hours earlier he'd been at the top of his game. In his professional life, he was in line to step into the chief's position when Henderson moved on, and in his private life he had a beautiful wife and family, an expensive home in a prime location, money in the bank and was considered a pillar of the community. On top of that he'd lined up Suzie, who he considered the hottest young woman he'd ever set eyes on, to resume the sexual relations he'd enjoyed when he knew her as Gypsy Diamond. Sex on tap, he called that particular perk.

The deputy chief searched his memory for some sign that Suzie had been planning to set him up. Nothing came to him. He looked around for something to punch as his anger and frustration threatened to boil over.

In the hallway outside the office, Henderson was still deep in discussion with his two subordinates.

The younger officer asked, "Are you standing the deputy chief down immediately, Chief?"

Henderson nodded.

"Immediately."

"On full pay?" the same officer asked.

"On full pay," Henderson confirmed. "And tell him he is to have no contact with his accuser."

He eyeballed the young officer.

"*No* contact. Otherwise he'll do some jail time. Got it?"

"Got it, Chief."

When he saw there were no further questions, Henderson left his subordinates to carry out their orders. The pair returned to the chief's office.

27

Heading back to the meeting room he'd left Suzie in, Henderson turned his phone back on and saw that Barrett had phoned twice more. The official had left two voice messages for him. The chief didn't bother checking them. He could imagine their tone.

Upon arrival at the fourth floor, Henderson's phone rang. It was Barrett. Again.

"Art," the chief said, answering the call this time.

He had to hold the phone away from his ear as the council president loudly abused him.

As soon as Henderson could get a word in, he said, "Sorry I didn't phone back, Art. Damned phone died on me."

Calmer now, Barrett asked, "Have we made our little problem go away yet?"

"Not exactly."

"What–"

"Our preliminary investigation shows Deputy Chief Williams may have a case to answer to. I'm releasing him on cognizance."

"Does this need to go anywhere near the D.A.'s office?"

"I'm afraid it does."

There was silence over the phone as Barrett digested this.

The chief could well imagine what was going through the other's mind.

"Is that all, Art?"

"That's all, Paul."

Henderson ended the call.

28

Pausing outside the fourth floor meeting room, the chief glanced at the time on his phone's screen. It was just after midnight. He entered the room and found Suzie asleep on the couch, her head resting on a cushion and her face turned away from him.

Looking at her, he realized he was besieged by conflicted emotions. On the one hand, he was pissed that she'd wrecked his evening and had turned his department upside down with her brazen accusations; on the other hand, he was full of admiration for her. He considered her arrest of Williams a bold move.

In all his years with the department, it was the first citizen's arrest he'd ever witnessed and the first such arrest of a cop he'd ever heard of.

He looked at the back of Suzie's head.

"Gutsy bitch," he murmured with more than a hint of affection.

Suzie reminded him in no small way of his own daughter. His daughter was a similar age, too, and he could well imagine what she would think of the young woman asleep on the couch.

The chief gently shook Suzie's shoulder. It took two attempts to wake her.

"What?" Suzie asked groggily as she woke.

"Sorry to wake you," Henderson said.

Suzie roused herself and sat up slowly, wiping sleep from her eyes and adjusting her hair as best she could without the aid of a mirror.

"I'm very sorry we detained you for so long," Henderson said, sitting down on a chair opposite her.

"What time is it?"

"It's after midnight...Sorry about that."

Even half asleep, Suzie could sense Henderson's manner had softened. She took that as a good sign.

As if reading her mind, the chief said, "Your accusations stood up to initial scrutiny. A full investigation is underway as we speak and the case will be officially referred to the District Attorney first thing in the morning."

Suzie embraced the feeling of relief that flooded through her.

I got the bastard!

Smiling, she asked, "So I'm free to go?"

"You're free to go. Before you do, I must inform you of a few things."

He looked at her earnestly.

"There may well be a court case so please don't talk to anyone else about what you have been through. That includes media."

"Of course...Will I need to appear in court?"

"Most likely. Is that okay?"

"Yes," Suzie replied hesitantly.

She hadn't thought that far ahead. With so much going on, her entire focus had been on gathering evidence against Williams and executing a citizen's arrest that would stick. The thought of having to face her tormentor in court didn't exactly thrill her. And the knowledge that his abuse of her as well as her past indiscretions would inevitably be raised by the defense didn't bear thinking about.

"Oh, and I meant to tell you, there's someone waiting for you outside," Henderson said. "Andy Davis. He said to tell you he's in a blue Mercedes, which is parked opposite the front entrance. He's here to drive you back to your apartment." Smiling, the chief added, "He seems worried about you."

Suzie smiled. It warmed her to think a friendly face awaited her. She realized she needed a friend about now.

Henderson prepared to depart then hesitated.

"There's something else."

"Oh?"

29

Henderson leaned forward and earnestly grasped Suzie's hands in his.

"On behalf of the LAPD…I want you to know I am deeply sorry one of our officers caused you so much distress."

Suzie thought she saw Henderson's eyes glisten and she realized his words came from the heart.

The chief continued, "We can only ask your forgiveness."

Suzie nodded.

"Thank you for your apology, Chief Henderson."

That's the least I deserve, Buster.

Much as she appreciated his sentiments, she wasn't going to let him off the hook by forgiving the organization he headed for the degradation and stress she'd suffered at the hands of one of his closest colleagues.

"I will certainly consider your request."

Hiding his disappointment as best he could, Henderson released

Suzie's hands and headed for the door. He'd been hoping for some sort of closure. Her forgiveness would have provided that.

#

Suzie emerged from LAPD HQ to find herself surrounded by media. No-one had thought to warn her that reporters and film crews were camped outside the building, hoping to catch her when she emerged. She realized she shouldn't have been surprised by the media ambush. She was, after all, *the* big story of the day.

Ignoring the questions hungry reporters fired at her, she looked around for Davis. It took her a moment to spot him. His head was just visible through the driver's side window of his midnight blue *Merc*, which was parked a little way down on the other side of the street.

Suzie sprinted toward the car, the media reps following close behind. As she neared the car, she saw her chauffeur was asleep behind the wheel.

Davis woke with a start when Suzie flung open the front passenger door and jumped in next to him.

"Drive!" she ordered.

Only now did Davis notice the newshounds converging on the car.

"You got it!" he said, starting the engine.

They drove off with a squeal of tires. Behind them, photographers' flashbulbs lit up the night as reporters' questions were blown away in the car's slipstream.

Soon, Suzie and Davis were both laughing. The absurdity of the occasion had dawned on each simultaneously.

30

"What a night!" Suzie remarked.

"What a night indeed," Davis agreed.

Smiling, he looked in the rearview mirror to ensure they weren't being followed then pulled the *Merc* over onto the side of the street.

"You're a dark horse," he said, turning off the engine. "One minute you're on sick leave, next minute you're arresting a cop... And not just any cop... The LAPD's Deputy Chief of Police for Christ's sake!"

"How did you hear about it?" Suzie asked.

"Hear about it? I saw it on CNN... And the airwaves have been full of your evening's exploits."

As if to prove his point, Davis turned on the car radio. Surfing the stations, he settled on L.A. talk station Radio *KFI-AM*. Late night host Kevin Harris was talking to a young female caller.

"My friend said the Fox girl was brilliant!" the caller said.

"Your friend saw it?" Harris asked. "What was he doing there?"

"*She,*" the caller corrected him. "She was one of the mayor's voluntary election campaign canvassers and was there by official invitation... like the Fox girl... and she saw the whole thing. She said it was the gutsiest thing she ever saw."

"Did she say how the police reacted when she...um...when Susan Fox handcuffed the Deputy Chief Williams?"

"Yeah, she said he looked like he wanted to kill her. He was furious."

Behind the Merc's wheel, Davis said, "Wish I'd been there to see that."

"I wished you were there, too," Suzie said. "I was freaking out... Could've done with an ally about then."

"I bet."

Over the airwaves, radio talk host Kevin Harris welcomed another caller – a well-spoken, middle-aged, professional woman who introduced herself as Carol.

"Carol, you're the twentieth caller to phone in tonight about the citizen's arrest, and all but one of the calls have been from women," Harris said. "I guess it's correct to say Susan Fox's actions tonight have resonated with the fairer sex..."

"Very much so, Kevin," the caller said. "Miss Fox's actions certainly resonated with me!"

"You and a lot of others by the sound of it... I know you can't speak for all the other women out there Carol, but can you put it into words how what went down earlier tonight impacted on you personally?"

"Well, I wasn't there of course...so I am only going on what I've heard on the radio and the snippet I saw on TV... I think what Miss Fox did was very brave and showed great initiative."

"Hear, hear," Davis murmured.

Warming to the subject, Carol continued, "I think what resonated with me, and no doubt with a lot of other women, was the fact that here's a wonderful example of a woman fighting back against sexual abuse. The fact that the abuser in this case is a senior police officer makes it all the more incredible."

"And newsworthy," Harris said.

"Of course…and that's a good thing."

"Oh?"

"Yes. The media has been full of reports lately on powerful men abusing young women and having their way with them… First we were deluged with reports on the control Harvey Weinstein exercised over starlets and other women. Then a convicted pedophile like Jeffrey Epstein hits the headlines with murky accounts of how he groomed underage girls for sex, not only for himself but for the likes of Prince Andrew and other wealthy friends… and that's just the tip of the iceberg by all accounts."

"Your point?" Harris prompted.

"*My point* is now we have an example of a young woman who has been a victim of –"

"We don't know if Susan Fox is the victim in this case," the talk host reminded his caller.

"No, we don't," Carol agreed. "But regardless, whether she is or isn't, her actions tonight will inspire women everywhere to fight back against abuse… I imagine members of the Me Too movement will use Miss Fox as a shining example of what women can achieve in the face of male domination, abuse and adversity."

"I couldn't put it better myself, Carol," Harris said. "Tell me, if Miss Fox was listening to this station now, what would you say to her?"

"I'd say, you go girl!"

"Okay Carol, thanks for your call."

Harris accepted a call from another caller.

31

Inside the *Merc*, Suzie reached out and switched off the radio.

Davis glanced at her.

"It's like that on all the stations," he said. "Everyone's talking about the incident and you're headlining all the news reports."

Suzie didn't respond.

"You okay?" Davis asked.

The young woman didn't answer immediately.

At length she said, "I didn't realize my actions would inspire other women to this extent."

"You better believe it. You heard what that woman said. You're a shining light...a wonderful example for the Me Too movement."

Suzie smiled. The thought that she might have inspired other women brought her some comfort and helped compensate for everything she'd endured.

Closing her eyes, she rested her head on the headrest. She just wanted to sleep.

Davis looked at her, suddenly concerned.

"You look exhausted…Let's get you home."

"Sounds good," Suzie murmured sleepily.

Davis started the engine and resumed driving the short distance up West 1st Street to Suzie's apartment complex.

Minutes later, they arrived at the complex to find it surrounded by waiting media. Reporters, photographers and camera crews milled around, waiting for the girl of the moment to appear. They came to life as soon as they saw her.

"Damn!" Suzie said. "I wasn't expecting this."

"The price of fame," Davis said. Thinking quickly, he added, "Don't take this the wrong way, but you're welcome to stay in my apartment until all this is over… In the spare room I mean."

Suzie's first instinct was to accept the invitation, but she assumed it would come with strings attached and she still wasn't ready to commit to a relationship.

"Thanks Andy, but I need familiar surroundings tonight."

Hiding his disappointment, Davis said, "Okay, but I insist on escorting you to your apartment. You'll need help getting past the media horde."

Suzie agreed to his suggestion and she was glad she did because bypassing the waiting horde proved easier said than done. More than once Davis had to physically restrain a reporter or photographer who became too insistent. It was a repetition of what Suzie had experienced at LAPD HQ and at the *Sheraton Grand* before that.

When they finally reached Suzie's floor they were both grateful to see they had it to themselves for the moment.

Stopping at her apartment door, she turned to Davis.

"You're a lifesaver, Andy. Thanks."

"No problem," he said.

"Goodnight," Suzie said.

She went to kiss his cheek, but he turned so that his lips met hers.

Suzie responded, but only for a moment. She broke contact and pushed him away.

"Too soon?" Davis asked, his eyes twinkling mischievously.

"Too soon," Suzie confirmed. "And too sneaky."

Smiling good-naturedly, she turned her back on him, unlocked her apartment door and disappeared inside.

Davis waited until he heard the door lock and then he departed, whistling to himself.

Inside her apartment, Suzie leaned back against the door. She thought about what had just transpired and part of her regretted she hadn't invited her protector inside.

"Part of me needs to eat and sleep, too," she reminded herself, noting it was now well after one in the morning.

Hurrying through to the kitchen, she grabbed a late night snack, which she wolfed down to appease her rumbling tummy. Before crashing, she had the foresight to turn off her smartphone and disconnect her landline.

She was asleep as soon as her head hit the pillow.

32

Two hours later, in the upmarket neighborhood of Glendale, a disgraced Heck Williams arrived by private vehicle outside his gated home, having been processed and released on cognizance after being stood down on full pay. He arrived to find a small crowd of media representatives, including at least one television news film crew, waiting for him outside the front gate.

The media reps sprang to life as soon as they saw the deputy chief.

Ignoring the questions reporters fired at him, he used his remote to open the front gates and then quickly drove through the gates, automatically closing them behind him.

Williams cursed when at the end of the long drive he saw a black *Range Rover* he recognized parked outside the front door of his two-storied house. It belonged to his father-in-law the Governor.

"Fuck me!" he muttered, banging the top of the steering wheel with both hands.

Since departing LAPD HQ, he'd been rehearsing what he was going to say to his wife who he knew would be beside herself after what had gone down. Now he realized he'd have his influential in-law to contend with as well.

As he pulled up alongside the Governor's vehicle, the front door of the house opened and Williams saw his wife Pamela step out onto the verandah. She had obviously been crying; her face was tear-stained and drawn; she was still in her day clothes and clearly hadn't slept even though it was after three in the morning.

The most disconcerting sight, however, was the Governor. He was standing at his daughter's shoulder and his face looked like thunder.

Williams was tempted to drive off the property and keep on driving.

For possibly the hundredth time since the citizen's arrest, he cursed Suzie Fox.

33

Suzie didn't wake until ten on Saturday morning. She felt totally refreshed, having enjoyed her first good sleep in over a week.

At first, she couldn't remember the events of the previous night. She just remembered crashing late.

Slowly, as sleep faded and she became alert, it all came back to her.

"I did it!" she murmured. "I got the bastard!"

Yawning, she stretched, luxuriating in the feeling of contentment that enveloped her. It felt so good after the stress and tension she'd been under this past week.

Retrieving her smartphone from a bedside cabinet, she turned it on to discover there were thirty-four voice messages awaiting her and even more texts. A quick check revealed the messages were from news reporters, work colleagues, friends and others. It was a sobering reminder she was the big news of the moment.

One of the phone messages and two of the texts, she noticed, were from Davis.

You don't quit do you, Andy?

She smiled as she realized she was enjoying the attention the New Yorker was paying her.

Suzie turned the phone off again. She needed more time to herself to process things before speaking to every Tom, Dick and Andy.

After preparing a hearty cooked breakfast – her first breakfast to speak of in the past week – she sat down to enjoy it in front of her laptop. Intent on catching up on the latest news, she checked online news sites. At the same time, she kept one eye on her television set, which she'd tuned into *CNN News*, and one ear on the radio, which conveniently happened to be on *The Answer AM 870* news station.

Clicking on the *Los Angeles Times Online* site, she saw the entire front page had been devoted to the previous night's citizen's arrest. She noticed her court reporter friend Mel Harper had one of two bylines on the story.

The article featured a three-column photograph showing Williams and herself standing together, shackled as they were by the handcuffs which were clearly visible. The big cop towered over her, the expression on his face leaving onlookers in no doubt what he was thinking. The article, which was headed *Young woman makes citizen's arrest of LAPD Deputy Chief at mayoral function*, carried over to page three, which was entirely devoted to the same incident.

The front-page subheading for the same article was even more explosive. It read: *Arrested cop pleads his innocence to charges of blackmail, extortion and threatened rape.*

Several paragraphs had been bolded and Suzie's eyes were drawn to these.

Reciting them aloud, she murmured, "Deputy Chief Williams was the subject of a citizen's arrest carried out last night by Los Angeles resident Susan Fox. In a move described by many as courageous, Miss Fox apprehended the senior police officer in front of guests at a mayoral function at the Sheraton Grand Hotel. She was aided in this by none other than Los Angeles' newly re-elected Mayor, Dean Lopez. Mayor Lopez spoke up for Miss Fox, essentially forcing other LAPD officers in attendance to agree to her insistence the charges be taken seriously and Williams be taken into custody."

As she read the article, she found herself reliving the events of the previous evening. It almost felt as if she was reading about the exploits of someone else so surreal was it.

The article concluded:

> An LAPD spokesperson said today that Deputy Chief Williams, who was released last night on cognizance and subject to further investigation, has been temporarily relieved of his duties and stood down on full pay. The spokesperson says the deputy chief strenuously denies the accusations leveled at him.
>
> Meanwhile, the District Attorney is considering whether the accused has a case to answer for. His decision will determine whether the case goes to trial.

News that Williams had denied the accusations didn't surprise Suzie, but the revelation that he'd been released did and it left her feeling somewhat disturbed. She hadn't yet caught up with the news that he'd returned home, and she hoped he wasn't planning to pay her a visit. Logic told her he'd keep a low profile given the intense media scrutiny he was under, but even so the thought lingered.

A replay of the citizen's arrest screening on television caught her eye. It began at the point she retrieved the package from her shoulder bag and announced to the whole world what it contained. A male newsreader was speaking off screen, but the volume was too low for her to hear what he was saying.

Using the TV remote, she turned up the volume in time to hear the newsreader say, "A spokesperson for the Los Angeles chapter of the Me Too movement said today Susan Fox displayed exceptional courage in the face of daunting odds and she deserves a medal. Women throughout America are praising Miss Fox's actions and she is seen by many as a shining light for the Me Too movement."

34

Suzie muted the TV volume and looked away.

Wow!

The newsreader's comments had given her a lot to think about.

She had no idea her actions might inspire other women. The realization some may see her as a role model for other young women, especially women who, like her, had been abused, suddenly empowered her. It really brought home the importance of what she'd achieved and it made her feel doubly proud of herself.

Suzie closed her eyes, lost in thought.

The young woman the whole world was now talking about found herself fighting back tears. It was as if all the emotion and turmoil of recent days had caught up with her.

A myriad of emotions coursed through her. She was happy to know she'd turned the tables on her nemesis and she was delighted her actions might have inspired others. At the same time she felt apprehensive about the likelihood she'd have to appear as the primary witness in some drawn-out, high profile court case. The knowledge that she'd have to lay her soul bare in a crowded courtroom filled her with trepidation.

My drug-taking and escort agency activities will become public knowledge. The defense lawyers will have a field day.

An even worse thought occurred.

The sexual abuse I suffered at the hands of my stepfather will all come out under cross-examination!

Suzie could feel past events catching up with her. She suddenly felt overwhelmed and couldn't stem the tears that had been threatening these past few minutes. They arrived in a flood and she was soon sobbing uncontrollably.

35

Despite her fears for the future, Suzie settled back into to her former life with less effort than she'd have thought possible considering what she'd been through – and considering she was now a national celebrity.

The young woman everyone was talking about had returned to her job at *Boutique PR* on the Monday morning following the extraordinary and well publicized event at the *Sheraton Grand*. Within a week, she'd been reinstated as the firm's account manager for *Chisholm Security* – much to the delight of Andy Davis who continued to pursue her.

Women's magazines ran articles on her, praising her for her actions in successfully executing a citizen's arrest of Williams; television networks and other media outlets constantly pressured her for interviews; women's organizations and victims' groups invited her to speak to their members; and members of the burgeoning *Me Too* movement embraced her as one of their own.

Suzie handled all the attention with good grace and with the maturity to be expected of a public relations exec. In fact, she was a promoter's dream even if she did turn down most of the interview requests and public speaking invitations she received.

Best of all, the nightmares and flashbacks she'd been experiencing since her teenage years subsided and then finally disappeared.

She was starting to feel like a new woman. So much so she thought she was closer to finally putting Davis out of his misery and agreeing to date him.

The only thing stopping her was the possible court case that was still hanging over her like a dark cloud.

36

The D.A. took two weeks to decide whether Williams had a case to answer to. When his decision was announced, there was a public uproar and Suzie didn't know whether to laugh or cry.

In his wisdom, the D.A. said the evidence compiled against the deputy chief was insufficient to justify prosecution. He referred to the accused's long and impressive track record in law enforcement and made reference to the secret recording supplied, which he described as *an element of entrapment by the deputy chief's accuser* and which he claimed *somewhat diluted the evidence.* The D.A. concluded by saying, *While the deputy chief's explanation for his actions was credible, his actions were perhaps unwise in the circumstances and undoubtedly caused Miss Fox unnecessary distress.*

Media response to the D.A.'s decision was predictably damning, and once again Suzie and the citizen's arrest she'd made of Williams were headline news. Talkback radio was taken over by irate callers who claimed the decision was part of a cover-up. More than one caller referred to the deputy chief's connection to the Governor.

Suzie was bombarded by requests for her comment on the decision.

She answered every request with a *No comment*. The truth was she didn't know how she felt. On the one hand she was disappointed Williams had been exonerated. On the other hand she was relieved she wouldn't have to endure a lengthy court case and have her dirty laundry aired.

A bigger bombshell was to follow.

37

Early in the week following the announcement of the D.A.'s decision, Deputy Chief Hector Williams was found dead inside his car in his garage at home. The car's engine had been left running and although no suicide note had been found, police said there were no suspicious circumstances.

News of the probable suicide followed reports that as well as being publicly vilified, Williams was being ostracized by his LAPD colleagues, his wife had filed for divorce and his high profile father-in-law, the Governor, had disowned him.

Mainstream media commentators, bloggers and citizen journos alike insisted that Williams had been driven to suicide by his public vilification. The overwhelming sentiment was that he wouldn't be missed. Furthermore, the universal consensus was that Williams was obviously guilty and had killed himself because his crimes had been exposed.

Suzie certainly shared that sentiment.

38

The young account exec learned of her nemesis' passing just before she left *Boutique PR* at the end of another workday.

Walking to her apartment complex, Suzie's thoughts turned to Andy Davis. He was fast becoming a fixture in her life even though they still hadn't dated. She saw him most days in a professional capacity and there was no doubt the brash New Yorker was growing on her.

With every passing day she realized she was developing stronger feelings for him. Feelings she never thought she'd be capable of experiencing again.

Now, with Williams out of her life and with no court case to worry about, she felt ready to enter into a relationship.

She smiled to herself as she experienced a delicious fluttering in her lower tummy.

It's time you enjoyed a man's company again, my girl.

Suzie retrieved her smartphone from her bag and speed-dialed Davis.

He answered straight away, asking "Are you still stalking me, Fox?"

"In your dreams, Davis," Suzie laughed. Before the young man could respond, she asked, "Does that dinner invitation still stand?"

"What dinner invitation?"

Suzie could picture him smiling mischievously.

"*That* dinner invitation… The one you've been pestering me about for weeks now."

"Oh, that one!"

This time they both laughed.

"Yes, that one!" Suzie said, smiling at a passerby who had obviously recognized her.

"Let me consult my diary," Davis said. "Well, what do ya know, I'm free tonight! Pick you up at eight, Fox?"

"Pick me up at eight, Davis."

Still smiling, Suzie terminated the call and returned her phone to her bag. She listened to the sounds of L.A. as she approached her apartment complex on West 1st Street. Carolers could be heard singing above the sounds of the peak-time traffic, reminding her and other pedestrians Christmas was only a week away.

Entering her building, she saw someone approaching out of the corner of her eye.

39

The girl looked like a street waif in her soiled sneakers and ill-fitting, unwashed jeans and sweatshirt. Suzie thought she looked about eighteen. She'd obviously been waiting for her.

Stopping in front of the ground floor elevator door, Suzie studied the girl as she neared. Her long, blond hair hung lank down to her bony shoulders and she had a haunted look about her. Suzie guessed she might be a prostitute or a junkie.

Or both perhaps.

The girl stopped in front of Suzie and flashed what might have passed as a smile, revealing two missing teeth in the process.

"I've been waiting for you," the girl said.

Suzie noted she spoke with a strong Southern twang.

"Do I know you?" Suzie asked.

The girl shook her head.

"You're Suzie Fox, aren't you?"

"Yes."

Suzie was certain the girl was about to ask her for money.

"What's your name?"

"That doesn't matter," the girl said. "I just wanted to thank you."

"Thank me? For what?"

"For saving my life."

Suzie stared at her opposite, unsure what she was getting at. She noticed the girl was crying now.

"I don't understand."

Ignoring the stares of other residents coming and going, she placed a caring hand on the girl's shoulder.

"I saw you arrest that cop on TV," the girl sobbed. "I was being abused, too, by my supplier" – Suzie guessed she was referring to her drug supplier – "and after I saw what you did I decided to kick my habit and get away from him."

Now Suzie understood. Looking into the girl's eyes, she saw desperation in them. She also saw hope and was suddenly reminded of herself at the same age.

"Tell me your name," she said.

"Jacqueline," the girl said, drying her eyes with the back of her hand. "But they call me Jacks." Sniffing, the girl known as Jacks continued, "You inspired me to turn my life around. I'm getting off the streets and going back to live with my parents... I couldn't have found the courage to do it if I hadn't seen what you did."

Jacks smiled for real this time. The smile lit up her whole face and revealed a hint that she might once have been pretty – and maybe still could look pretty with a bit of luck. The girl suddenly hugged Suzie and then ran outside before her heroine could respond.

40

Suzie went to follow Jacks, but decided to let her go. She became aware of the elevator door opening behind her. Entering the unoccupied elevator, she was pleased that she had it to herself.

Ascending to her floor, she thought about Jacks and what she'd said.

She thanked me for saving her life!

The encounter brought home to her the impact her actions had had on others. She realized Jacks wasn't the only girl out there who had been inspired by her courage.

Suzie suddenly felt ready for whatever the New Year brought her way. As well as inspiring others, her recent experience had given her an inner strength she never knew she had.

She smiled at herself when she noticed her reflection in the shiny elevator door.

You go girl!

The End

If you liked this story, the authors would greatly appreciate a review from you on Amazon.

Publisher's note:

For your reading pleasure we are pleased to include on the following pages the prologue and first three chapters of the critically acclaimed, female-led, epic murder mystery **SILENT FEAR (A novel inspired by true crimes),** *also by Lance & James Morcan...*

SILENT FEAR
(A novel inspired by true crimes)

Prologue

A solitary figure sweated profusely as he toiled away, unconcerned by the confined space of the basement he worked in or by the wooden floorboards that formed a ceiling just a metre or so above his head. Claustrophobia, it seemed, wasn't an issue. Stretched out full length on the concrete floor, he worked by the light of a torch he'd left resting beside him. His full attention was on filling a hole, brick by brick, in a wall that dissected one corner of the basement.

It was a painstakingly slow process. He was a thinker and a planner, not a bricklayer or labourer. Even so, he understood the basics of bricklaying and he was blessed with a certain amount of natural strength, and this was helping him now. To protect his hands, he wore a pair of snug-fitting, black, leather gloves not unlike driving gloves.

A little research was all it had taken to familiarise himself with the rudiments of bricklaying. The upshot was he used quick-mix cement. Three parts sand to one part masonry cement. That's what the supplier's instructions had stated, but he'd added an extra spadeful of cement for good measure because he felt it needed that.

The instructions also advised using fine-grade masonry sand and fresh masonry cement preferably from an unopened bag. That he hadn't managed because he didn't want to be seen purchasing the product, and so he'd had to use what was available. And what was available was a half-used bag of course-grade masonry. Touch wood, it was doing the job – so far at least.

"Mix only what you need" the instructions had read. He'd estimated half a wheelbarrow-full would do it with some to spare, so that's the amount he'd mixed. Because of the basement's low head-clearance, he'd had to pour the mixture into buckets – six of them – and drag them one at a time to his cramped workplace.

Two extra trips had been required, including one to fetch a bucket of water. He was using the water to keep the cement from setting before applying it. The other trip had involved dragging the object he was now concealing from a room on the lower floor of the building directly above his head. That had required the most effort as the object weighed almost as much as he did.

The instructions had also recommended the addition of lime to the mixture – "to bond and strengthen the stonework you are building," according to the supplier's instructions. He didn't have any lime, and that had bothered him initially. Now, as he saw how well the cement was bonding with the bricks, he relaxed a little. *Easy*, he thought. *Like falling off a bike.*

He was quite proud of his trowelling technique. It improved with the laying of each brick, but it was tricky and he found he had to focus.

"Hold the trowel at a ninety degree angle," he'd been advised, but he had quickly discovered ninety degrees was a bit too ambitious in the confined space. It wasn't as if he could work standing up. Lying down, seventy degrees or thereabouts was the best he could manage with the trowel, but that was sufficient.

The main challenge, he'd discovered, was ensuring the quick-mix cement in the buckets didn't set before he could apply it. Premature setting was only avoided by regular application of water, which he dispensed by using his trowel to transfer small amounts from the water bucket to the other buckets and then giving their contents a good stir. It required some effort, and despite the basement's cool temperature he found he was sweating more with each passing minute.

Ever so gradually the hole in the brick wall grew smaller as he laid more bricks.

Despite what was at stake, he worked at a leisurely pace, all the while thinking. That was something he did a lot these days. Thinking, that is.

The hole was now so small he could hardly see the object he was concealing. Only the deceased's face was visible, covered by the transparent plastic bag he'd used so effectively to cut off the other's air supply just thirty minutes earlier.

He smiled at the memory of the deceased's final moments. Those last seconds when the young man had recognised his attacker and realised he was about to die.

Beautiful...poetry in motion...slow motion.

Oh how he loved the exhilarating, orgasmic-like feelings he'd experienced as the life of another was snuffed out. He willingly embraced them as he relived the moment. It was as if the helpless young man before him was still dying.

Studying the deceased now, or what he could still see of him at least, he recalled how he'd laughed uproariously just before death came to his victim. The visuals replayed over and over in his mind. He remembered how the veins in the young man's eyeballs, face and neck appeared to burst as he was deprived of air, and how fragile he'd looked – like a child being tortured.

The icing on the cake had been when he'd used his hands to communicate a final message via sign language. He could still see the look on his victim's face when, seconds before death came, he realised what was being communicated to him. It was a look of total horror, which was somehow more accentuated when viewed through the transparent plastic bag. That had made this killing even more satisfying.

What he had communicated was simple yet definitive: "Game over!"

As he relived what happened, it felt like every cell in his body was jumping for joy. It was as if his very DNA had been created for one purpose and one purpose only: to kill.

He had been planning the murder these past six months. In fact, he'd first thought of killing him years ago, but it required time for those thoughts to solidify into a plan – a concrete plan in more ways than one.

Now that he'd acted, he wondered why it had taken him so long. It wasn't as if he was afraid or anything like that. He'd delayed because he couldn't decide exactly how he wanted the young man to die. Bludgeoning, shooting, stabbing, poisoning, gassing, drowning had all been considered. Finally, he'd opted for suffocation. Why? He couldn't really say. Certainly he wanted to watch him suffer. And he wanted to prolong his suffering. But stabbing or poisoning or any number of methodologies could have achieved that.

Looking at him now, the killer knew he'd made the right decision. The deceased's tortured face seemed distorted inside the plastic bag that covered his head, and his sightless eyes still registered the intense fear he'd experienced in his final ghastly moments.

Studying him in the torchlight, he felt his manhood hardening beneath him. He removed one of his gloves then, raising his pelvis off the floor, he reached down and began pleasuring himself, all the while looking at his victim.

Satisfaction arrived quickly and he groaned as he came.

Recovering his composure, he donned his glove and resumed working.

It wasn't long before the hole was completely bricked over. He shone his torch on the wall and inspected his handiwork.

Perfect.

The newly laid bricks aligned flawlessly with the older bricks. That was no accident because he'd used identical surplus bricks the building's owner had thoughtfully left in the basement. Finally, he cleaned up, removed his gloves and then began crawling back the way he'd come, taking his buckets and work tools with him.

As he departed, he knew he'd need to kill again. And soon. He *had* to experience those wonderful feelings again.

He was confident he wouldn't have long to wait; his master plan was already in motion.

1

London, like the rest of England and most of Western Europe, was unseasonably hot. Summer had only officially arrived a week ago and already the capital's maximum temperatures had topped 29°C. Forecasters were predicting the nation's record high of 38.5 would topple before summer was over.

On this particular weeknight, in West London's Royal Borough of Kensington and Chelsea, the pubs and bars were full to overflowing as office workers and residents mingled over a few drinks of the alcoholic variety as they endeavoured to assuage their thirst.

In the posh district of South Kensington, not far from Old Brompton Road and only ten minutes' walk north to Hyde Park or fifteen minutes south to the River Thames, take your pick, an elderly gent emerged from his favourite local bar and weaved his way unsteadily across a busy street. He'd clearly had one or two drinks too many.

The old man came to the attention of a passing cop a few minutes later when he stopped to address the larger-than-life statue of Lord Chester Wandsworth, which towered over the entrance of the university he founded more than a decade earlier.

Wandsworth University was no ordinary educational institution. It was a university for the deaf community. Correction. It was *the* university for the deaf community – in Britain at least, and, if those responsible for the running of similar institutions elsewhere were honest, it was probably *the* university for the deaf community anywhere. Its student fees certainly reflected that, and it attracted deaf and hard of hearing students from throughout the world.

Lord Wandsworth was no ordinary individual either. Partially deaf, he took it upon himself to champion deaf students and see to it that they had the same education opportunities as those of normal hearing. The end result of this benefactor's generosity was a state-of-the-art educational facility whose stellar reputation was known and admired worldwide.

Unfortunately, Lord Wandsworth was in no condition to enjoy the fruits of his generosity. Since suffering a serious brain injury in a horse-riding accident, the good lord had been confined to bed at his private estate in South Cambridgeshire. But his statue at least continued to watch over the university 24/7.

Looking up at the effigy, the elderly bar patron had no idea the gentleman it was named after was still alive. Not surprising given death usually comes before the commissioning of a statue in someone's honour. Such was Lord Wandsworth's reputation and popularity the tribute had been fast-tracked.

The bar patron usually had a word for Lord Wandsworth on those evenings his wife allowed him out for a tipple, and tonight was no different except that he'd imbibed more than was customary and so was somewhat more talkative than usual. "I've always looked up to you, guv," he shouted, looking up at the stern, stony features of the man he addressed. "But then… I s'pose everyone looks up to you." He chuckled at his attempt at humour and nearly fell over when he stepped back into the gutter.

"Are you alright, sir?" a gruff voice enquired.

The elderly gent turned around to see a police car had pulled up nearby. The driver, a fresh-faced young cop, asked again if he was alright.

"Aye, I'm fine," the old man assured him. Not wanting to get offside with the law, he resumed his homeward journey, bidding both the cop and Lord Wandsworth a good evening as he went his merry way.

The cop watched the gent's progress for a moment before gazing up at the impressive statue and the even more impressive multi-storied campus building behind it.

Wandsworth University was six storeys high and spanned the length of one entire block. Its top floor was ablaze with lights, and the silhouettes of its occupants could be seen at many of the windows.

The cop took one last look at the building then drove off. He drove with all the windows down, preferring natural ventilation to air-conditioning to cope with the evening's heat and with the humidity that accompanied it.

#

In Wandsworth University's student common room young, trendy, deaf students of various nationalities chilled out, played pool and watched television. Others ate at a bistro at the far end of the crowded room. Their lightweight attire left no doubt they, too, were feeling the heat.

Most conversed in sign language, their hand signs almost too fast for the eye to follow. Some wore hearing aids, others high-tech cochlear implants. Some even conversed in spoken language while those who were profoundly deaf either relied on their devices or sign language to communicate. More than a few flirted with each other, as to be expected in a gathering of so many young singles.

They were a mixed lot, ranging in age from late teens to mid-thirties, and they were in the main from well-heeled families. They had to be well off to afford the steep fees. There were exceptions, however. Some of the students were sponsored – most by charitable institutions in their own city or country, and a few by Wandsworth University itself by way of scholarships. Lord Wandsworth had expressed a desire that well deserving students from lower socio-economic backgrounds be accommodated as much as possible, and the uni's board members had honoured that to the best of their ability, or to the extent their budget allowed at least.

A casual observer wouldn't have picked it, but the normally animated students were more subdued than usual. And it wasn't because of the oppressive heat. They, along with the rest of the nation, had received concerning news in recent days.

Many crowded around a big screen television set, watching a *BBC* news report and reading the subtitles that ran along the bottom of the screen as the newsreader delivered the latest sobering instalment of news.

"The World Health Organisation reports the death toll from the Monkey Flu virus has risen to twenty thousand worldwide," the newsreader said.

More students stopped to watch, engrossed, as disturbing images from around the world flashed across the screen.

Off screen, the newsreader continued, "Although still in its early stages, the pandemic is already more potent than the 2009 Swine Flu outbreak."

Images included overcrowded New York hospital wards, mass cremations in Mumbai, emergency medical meetings in Moscow, mass burials in Cape Town, panicked citizens wearing face masks in some unnamed Latin American country, sheet-covered bodies on stretchers lining hospital corridors somewhere in Australia, and the bodies of victims being wheeled into Tokyo morgues.

Still off screen, the newsreader said, "In addition to severe flu symptoms, those who contract the virus suffer blurred vision, which almost invariably leads to blindness."

The *BBC* news report then cut to distressed Monkey Flu patients in a hospital ward in Brussels. Most of those in the foreground were looking straight at camera and many seemed to have a white film over the pupils of their eyes. Some appeared to be blind. It made for difficult viewing and some students had to look away. For members of the deaf community, blindness was something too awful to consider.

The newsreader continued, "World Health Organisation doctors describe the alarming symptom as a never-before-seen flu ailment and a type of ON, or Optic Neuritis, which is inflammation of the optic nerve and is often associated with multiple sclerosis. Unlike regular Optic Neuritis, many victims display cloudy, cataract-like symptoms in their eyes and invariably end up blind."

Wandsworth's dapper fifty-year-old chancellor Ron Fairbrother chose this moment to enter the room. A tall, distinguished-looking West Indian Brit, immaculately dressed with fashionable glasses and a hearing aid, Fairbrother acknowledged his students as he joined them to watch the news. The personable chancellor's sudden arrival was nothing out of the ordinary. His management style was very hands on, and he regularly mixed with students and staff in and out of normal working hours.

"No cases of Monkey Flu have been reported in the UK," the newsreader continued. "The Secretary of State for Health attributes this to the rigid anti-virus strategies in place."

Britain's Secretary of State for Health appeared onscreen, looking slightly anxious, but determined. "We are one of the few countries left without a single confirmed case of the virus," the stressed official said. "This is likely the result of our decision to close the UK's borders before any other nation in the world. You'll recall this unpopular move was referred to by some media as paranoid or alarmist, but even they can now see it was the right decision."

The newsreader reappeared onscreen and resumed speaking to camera. "Massive disruptions are continuing as a result of the government's decision to seal off our borders. Tens of thousands of British citizens remain stranded overseas due to the ban on all arrivals into the UK."

The ban was especially sobering for some of the students. A few British students had parents who were overseas on holiday or on business, and some foreign students had relatives who had been preparing to fly to London to visit them. For students directly affected – especially for those away from home for the first time – the closed borders policy was an ongoing concern.

Fairbrother could see the news was negatively impacting on some of the assembled. The chancellor inserted himself in the eye-line of students and waved his arms overhead. Most caught the movement and gave him their attention. Signing, Fairbrother advised them he was hopeful the flu pandemic would soon run its course. "I am confident the international travel ban will soon be lifted," he signed. He repeated himself, using regular speech for the benefit of those with hearing aids who may not have been able to see him. His perfect English hinted at his privileged upbringing and his university education. Smiling, he added, "Meanwhile… stay positive."

Not all the students were convinced, but for Fairbrother's sake they generally greeted his positivity with smiles.

There was little doubt the chancellor was popular. He had a reputation for being strict but fair, and his friendly, hands on approach endeared him to students and staff alike.

Satisfied he'd given the students some small measure of comfort, Fairbrother departed the room.

#

As midnight came and went, Wandsworth University's residents – most of them at least – slept. Those residents included students and staff members who occupied the uni's residential quarters on allocated floors.

Among those still awake was Welsh student Jamie Lewis, who, in the privacy of his room in the resident male students' quarters, was typing an email on his laptop at his desk. The nuggetty twenty-one-year-old was drafting a weekly report for his parents. They liked to be kept informed about what he was up to. Jamie, an only child, was close to his parents, so it was no chore at all to keep in touch regularly.

The room was snug but well appointed. Identical to the others on the floor – and near-identical to the rooms in the female quarters on the floor above – it was fully carpeted and comprised a single bed, bedside table, desk and chair, free-standing wardrobe and a bookshelf, which, in this room at least, was fully stocked. All the books bar one were reflective of the subjects Jamie was studying, the one exception being a book on Welsh rugby, his big passion. In his hometown Cardiff he'd played rugby through all the junior and senior grades at school, and here at Wandsworth he was considered a sitter to crack the uni's First Fifteen in the coming winter.

Not surprisingly, one entire wall was decorated with posters and photos of the Welsh rugby team, including action shots of his favourite players.

Deaf since birth, Jamie was one of a number of students enrolled at Wandsworth who was considering whether to receive a CI, or cochlear implant – that miraculous electronic medical device, which, in theory at least, allows a deaf person to hear. Jamie's parents were very keen for him to receive a CI, but he was in two minds. He was mindful the CI issue was highly political in the deaf community, and deaf adults who received an implant were sometimes perceived as traitors and shut out of that community. The political tension that existed between CI surgeons and the deaf populace – in the recent past at least – was legendary. Jamie had witnessed some of that tension first hand, and he wasn't at all sure he wanted to receive an implant. He was happy as he was.

That's what he was trying to relay to his parents by email. It wasn't easy. They were convinced a CI would be the solution for his *problem*, as they somewhat insensitively called his deafness.

The specialists said he was profoundly deaf, but he wasn't certain that diagnosis was one hundred percent correct: he suffered tinnitus, and regularly heard the sounds associated with that annoying condition. Those sounds included a ringing, whistling, hissing, buzzing and even chirping on occasion. The tinnitus was intermittent, sometimes disappearing for days on end, and in between bouts his inner world was reduced to a deathly silence – as was the case now. Even then, though, he often imagined he heard something. Or perhaps it was just wishful thinking.

Jamie was so engrossed in his typing, he didn't notice the handle of the unlocked door behind him slowly turn. If he had, he'd have seen the door open a few inches and he'd have seen a gloved hand on the handle. The glove was black leather fashioned in the style of snug-fitting driving gloves.

A male intruder entered the room. He wore a lightweight, hoodie-style sweatshirt with the hood all but concealing his face, and he carried a shoulder bag in one hand.

The intruder carefully closed the door behind him, locked it and then stepped behind the free-standing wardrobe.

Some sixth sense made Jamie look around. All seemed normal and he returned to his email.

Still behind the wardrobe, the intruder reached into his bag and drew out a steel claw hammer. In three quick strides he was right behind Jamie.

Only now as the intruder's shadow covered the desktop did the Welsh student realise he wasn't alone. Surprised, he spun around too late to avoid the hammer the intruder brought down on his head. The blow was delivered with sufficient force to knock Jamie out. Senseless, he slumped forward in his chair, his bloodied forehead coming to rest on the laptop's keyboard.

Jamie's attacker glanced up at the smoke alarm on the ceiling above the bed. He climbed onto the bed, reached up and disabled the alarm before returning to his victim's side. Then he reached into his bag again and pulled out a tin of lighter fluid and two blue ear candles of the type used for outer-ear hygiene. He unscrewed the tin's cap and doused the still unconscious student before returning the now empty tin to his bag. Next, he inserted the candles in Jamie's ears and then, as calm as you like, he removed the glove from his right hand, reached down inside the tracksuit pants he wore and began fondling himself.

The sadistic intruder was soon groaning with pleasure, and he came quickly.

A fluttering of the eyelids signalled that Jamie was regaining consciousness so the intruder donned his discarded glove, reached into his bag yet again and pulled out a length of rope and a scarf. The latter item he used to gag his victim, the former to tie him to the chair. His actions were clinical and efficient. It was as if he'd rehearsed this a thousand times. In fact, he had – in his mind at least. He wasn't one to leave anything to chance and, in the days and weeks leading up to this moment, he'd thought of little else.

Without further ado, he pulled a lighter from his pocket and lit each candle. He became momentarily mesmerised by the dancing flames, cocking his head as if awaiting some reaction from the now semi-conscious student. There was no reaction for the moment. Not that he noticed at least.

Finally, Jamie moaned as the candles burned down closer to his ears. Fumes rose from the lighter fluid and then ignited with a *whoosh*. It took a few moments before the student became aware he was gagged, tied up and on fire.

The intruder watched, entranced, as his victim struggled to escape the flames that enveloped him and the bonds that tied him to the chair.

Jamie was now writhing in agony. The flames were fierce and his skin was visibly blackening by the second. Such was his desperation, he overbalanced in the chair he was tied to and ended up on his back on the floor. He now resembled a fireball. A human fireball. So hot was it that his attacker had to take two steps backwards.

The intruder became excited and felt himself hardening again as he observed his victim's pain and terror. Jamie was now in his death throes, and his movements, so vigorous a few seconds ago, were slowing with every passing moment.

For the intruder, the need to make haste and quit the scene suddenly became the priority. He'd been here long enough. He lifted his shoulder bag from where he'd left it on the bed and took a final look around the smoky room. He was anxious not to leave behind any DNA or other evidence that could incriminate him.

By this time Jamie was unrecognisable and very dead.

Satisfied he'd overlooked nothing – the leather gloves he wore meant he didn't have to worry about leaving any fingerprints behind – Jamie's killer signed "Game over, asshole" to the still burning body before turning the light switch off and departing the room.

2

Valerie Crowther feigned exasperation as she allowed her deaf mother to brush a stray hair from the shoulder of her casual blazer in the dining room of the central London apartment they shared. "Don't fuss so, mother," Valerie communicated via sign language. She used one hand only. Her other hand was otherwise occupied, balancing an early morning cup of tea, which she valiantly tried to drink without spilling.

"Don't complain," her mother signed back.

It was a ritual they went through whenever Valerie was about to leave for work regardless of which shift she'd drawn. This was one of several comfortable routines they'd fallen into in the three years since Edith had sold her rural Oxfordshire home and relocated to live with her daughter.

The living arrangement suited both women. It suited Edith because she'd missed her daughter ever since her Val left home as a twenty-one-year-old to pursue a career in law enforcement, and it suited Valerie because her apartment had suddenly seemed empty after she separated from her husband of seven years. *The old seven-year-itch syndrome* – that was the reason she offered to anyone who asked why her marriage failed. Exactly whose itch it was she only ever divulged to her closest confidants.

"I must fly," Valerie signed, draining her cup and picking up her iPad, briefcase and a bundle of documents. She cursed when she dropped her iPad on the carpet. Her mother stooped to pick it up, but recoiled when she saw the gory image of a badly burnt, very dead Jamie Lewis on the screen. Barely recognisable as a human being, his face was grotesquely contorted into a frozen grin.

Only now did Valerie remember she left the iPad on after receiving the call from her superior. The call came just before breakfast. It turned out the student's body had been discovered only a short time earlier by a friend. The two students had scheduled an early morning run the previous evening. She quickly picked the iPad up and switched off the screen.

Valerie offered no explanation for the gruesome image to her mother, and Edith pretended she hadn't seen it.

At length, Edith signed, "Be careful, my dear." She worried so for her daughter's wellbeing as she was ever-mindful of the dangers of her chosen profession, but for her sake she always tried to remain bright and breezy.

"I will," Valerie signed with some difficulty as her hands were now rather full. She noticed her mother had become distracted. The older woman was looking at a framed photograph of her late husband, which occupied pride of place on the dining room mantelpiece.

Edith turned back to her daughter and signed, "Your father would be very proud of you."

Valerie glanced at the photo and the father she'd never known, or couldn't remember at least. A smiling, handsome-looking, thirty-five-year-old Doug Crowther stared back at her. His was an image his daughter and only child often studied. It was coming up thirty-two years since the heart attack that had so cruelly and unexpectedly taken him from them. She was only two at the time.

Edith smiled and signed, "You are a chip off the old block, my dear." Her eyes glistened with emotion.

Valerie didn't share her mother's sentimentality where the Late Doug Crowther was concerned. She'd never known him. She'd never known what it was like to have a father so never allowed herself the luxury of dwelling on something she'd never had, or couldn't remember at least. Not in her childhood, not now, not ever.

Valerie quickly signed, "Don't forget your pills, mother." She turned to leave, then, remembering the radio was still on in the kitchen, she hurried through to turn it off. It was of no use to Edith. Before switching it off, she caught the tail-end of a news report.

"Monkey Flu is believed to be considerably more virulent than the recent Ebola virus strain that broke out in Sudan earlier this year," the newsreader said. "Meanwhile, a World Health Organisation spokesperson said today the search continues to develop an effective vaccine to combat this new flu strain, which is also known by the scientific classification, H7N7. Experts say–" Valerie switched the radio off, waved goodbye to her mother and then hurried out the door.

A minute later, from the dining room window, a wistful Edith watched her daughter drive off in an unmarked police car. Everything about Valerie filled her with pride. She looked back at her dear departed husband as it occurred to her that in the photo, Doug was barely a year older than their thirty-four-year-old daughter. How she wished he was around to see their Val today.

Remembering her pills, Edith walked through to the bathroom, selected four colourful tablets – two from two different bottles – and downed them with a glass of water. It was a ritual she performed twice daily.

3

If London's streets were any quieter than usual, Valerie didn't notice. The early morning rush hour seemed as chaotic as ever with eternal traffic jams and streets clogged with people driving, cycling and walking to work. Their summery attire signalled another hot day was on the way.

Valerie was in work mode now. Behind the wheel of her police car she was no longer *plain* Valerie Crowther, divorcee and only child. She was First Class Detective Superintendent Crowther, of the Metropolitan Police, or *the Met*, as most refer to it. And no ordinary detective superintendent either: she was one of the few detectives on any of Britain's police branches fluent in British Sign Language, or BSL as it's commonly known. As a Coda, or child of a deaf adult, she had a big advantage over most others in the force who were called on to investigate crimes involving the deaf and hard of hearing. It was an advantage she'd been quick to use as and when required, and as a result her specialised services were in quite frequent demand.

Pulling up at a set of traffic lights on the Brompton Road section of the A4, the detective became aware she was under observation from the male driver of a late model Jaguar who had stopped alongside her. She didn't let on she knew she was being observed.

Valerie was used to being an object of attention. Tall and lithe with jet black hair, striking violet eyes and pale, porcelain-like skin, she had a natural beauty that allowed her the luxury of using the barest essentials when it came to cosmetics. This suited her profession, and she'd often go makeup-free, or as close to, in order to avoid accidentally contaminating the crime scenes she regularly visited. An added bonus was the practice allowed her to sleep in an extra fifteen minutes before arising – something her female colleagues envied.

Just before the lights turned green, she looked to her right and fastened her striking violet eyes on the Jag's driver who turned out to be a pompous-looking, middle-aged, pinstripe-suited gent. When the lights changed she accelerated away. Glancing in her rear-vision mirror, she smiled to herself when she saw the driver trying to restart his car, which had apparently stalled on take-off.

Despite her good looks, Valerie was only mildly aware of her attraction to members of the opposite sex. It was something she rarely dwelled on. She considered there were more important things in life, such as making a success of her career, paying the bills and looking after her mother. Besides, her looks hadn't always helped her. Whilst training to become a detective, and even when starting out as a newly qualified detective constable, she felt her appearance was more a hindrance than a help, especially with her fellow detectives. Even as recently as a decade ago, the force was very much a man's world; females were a second class minority on the force, and pretty females were considered fair game by the dominant males. Still she survived, and, it's fair to say, she thrived. Her seniority and her reputation were a testament to that.

The detective was well aware her rapid rise within the force still rankled with some of her colleagues. She'd deliberately cultivated a no-nonsense – some would say intimidating – persona, but if that upset anyone that was their problem. As the only child of a deaf adult she'd had to grow up quickly, interpreting for Edith and taking on responsibilities at a very young age. Being a Coda had made her fiercely protective of her mother, and had also moulded her personality to suit taking on responsibilities beyond her years.

As she became caught up in a queue of traffic further west along the A4 at Cromwell Road, Valerie reached out and switched on the iPad she'd left next to her on the front passenger seat. Jamie Lewis's gory image reappeared on screen. As the only available detective proficient in sign language, she was the logical choice to head the investigation into the student's murder. She glanced at the image once more then turned the iPad over, and, as the traffic began moving once more, she switched on the car radio. On air, a female talkback host was discussing the headline news of the moment with a male caller.

"Monkey Flu should be called Malaysian Flu because scientists now know it originated there," the talkback host said.

"Right," the caller agreed. "I believe the confusion arose because monkeys in a Malaysian zoo exhibited similar symptoms to the first humans who contracted the virus." The caller continued, "The connection with monkeys has since been disproven, but the name stuck. In fact it originated in horses and birds then crossed over to humans."

"Yes, that's correct," the talkback host said, "and I just want to repeat for our listeners an official statement issued by the World Health Organisation on this matter... 'H7N7 is a subtype of equine Influenza A virus – a genus of Orthomyxovirus, which is the virus responsible for causing influenza.' The organisation goes on to say that 'H7N7 is comprised of the surface proteins Hemagglutinin 7 and Neuraminidase 7'… whatever all that means."

The host switched to a female caller.

"This particular equine-avian strain of H7N7 is a complete mystery," the well-spoken caller said. "H7N7 hasn't been observed in horses since the 1970's and epidemiologists are still uncertain about its sudden reappearance." She spoke authoritatively and sounded like she knew what she was talking about.

Valerie turned the volume up.

"It was observed by scientists in poultry earlier this year, but not in horses for over forty-five years," the woman said. "This means humans have not been exposed to this lineage of influenza since the Seventies. Therefore this particular strain hasn't been included in any human vaccines, and the likelihood of acquired immunity is minimal."

Valerie hadn't caught the caller's name, but thought she could be a scientist or a medical researcher. At the very least she sounded professional.

The caller continued, "Let's hope our nation's closed borders policy prevents any infected cases here in Britain because this unusual panzoonotic disease has the potential to become the worst pandemic humanity has ever faced. And it's all because the scientific community did not suspect its reappearance." She sounded impassioned. "None of us in the research sector were prepared for this strain of H7N7."

"Why is that exactly?" the talkback host asked in a tone that almost sounded accusatory.

"Well, most of us believed it had long since become extinct. Although we know how to defend against influenza, this particular strain appears to have the ability to alter the surface proteins at a faster rate than we can create antibodies for it."

Introducing another caller, the host said, "We now have Rick from Bristol on the line. He informs us he has a conspiracy theory about the Monkey Flu".

Rick from Bristol coughed and spluttered into the phone before finally talking. "Firstly, let me say that I'm not one of those bloody tinfoil hat-wearing bastards," he assured listeners.

"Please remember you are live on air, Rick," the host cautioned.

Undeterred, Rick from Bristol continued, "I do my research and I always keep an open mind. And after doing my research I can only conclude one thing... The elite want to reduce global population!" Still spluttering, he said, "The planet is overpopulated and this virus is their way of getting rid of half of us! I mean, think about it... In 2016, the World Organisation for Animal Health stated they believed the equine, meaning horse, strain of H7N7 was officially extinct... Now remember, all viral strains are kept in storage, so if a long-forgotten, forty-five year old strain all of a sudden reappears in the population like this, we must question how that's possible? Has it occurred organically in nature? Or was it leaked from some secret scientific laboratory somewhere?"

Valerie turned the radio off as she left the A4 to drive into the quieter streets of South Kensington. She'd heard enough from Rick from Bristol for one day.

It wasn't long before Wandsworth University came into view. Though she had driven past it often enough she'd never had reason to visit it. Its size never failed to impress her, and she was looking forward to finally seeing what secrets it contained within its walls.

As she drew closer to the front entrance, she had to weave between stationary police cars, crime scene tape, clusters of curious onlookers, concerned students and jostling reporters. The murder of a deaf student was obviously big news.

More than once Valerie had to show her badge to law enforcement officers. They waved her through.

Finally, she found a spare parking space. Only as she turned off the ignition did she notice the ever-stern Lord Wandsworth looking down at her. The thought passed through her mind that he didn't look at all pleased by the latest turn of events. *Or perhaps the old boy doesn't like the look of me,* she wondered.

Climbing from the car, she mentally prepared herself for the inevitable onslaught of questions. The reporters and photographers had noticed her arrival and were converging on her.

Valerie avoided the media representatives with a curt "No comment" as she almost sprinted up the steps toward the entrance. Two burly, uniformed security men prevented her pursuers from following her through the front doors.

Inside, in the relative safety of the foyer, the first thing she noticed was that the temperature was cooler. Despite the early hour, the building's air-conditioning had already been turned on to combat the high temperatures forecast.

Valerie took stock of her surroundings. Wandsworth University was everything she'd expected and more. Its vastness and plushness couldn't fail to impress. The expensive furnishings and fittings were obvious clues to the institution's profitability, and all around students and staff members were going about their everyday business, albeit with an extra urgency given the tragedy that occurred overnight.

Directly ahead of her, two receptionists had their hands full trying to cope with a dozen or so people who all seemed to be talking or signing at once. Long corridors to the left and right of reception gave access to numerous ground floor facilities. Signs pointed to the chancellor's office, a conference room, meeting rooms, communications room, a communal café, gymnasium and indoor swimming pool. A swing door opened at the far end of the west wing corridor to reveal a full-size indoor pool.

Every room, she noted, was illuminated by expensive lighting, which was so startling it bordered on spectacular. She guessed this was as much to accommodate students who used sign language to communicate as it was to highlight the plush furnishings and show them off to the best effect.

Still more signs advertising various facilities on this and other floors caught her eye. They included *Lipspeaker UK lip-speaking support*, *Signworld Online BSL teaching materials*, *Definitely Theatre UK*, *Red Dot online video interpreting*, *Ai-Live captions and transcripts*, *Deaf Umbrella sign language interpreting*, *SignVideo online interpreting*, *121 Captions speech-to-text services*, *Phonak hearing acoustics*, *RAD financial advice for Deaf people* and *Bellman hearing loss solutions* to name but a few. The commercial overtones weren't lost on her. She could well imagine corporate sponsorship contributed significantly to Wandsworth's coffers.

Deaf students signed to each other as they walked by, and Valerie quickly established they were discussing the murder.

A group of male students drew near. Valerie noticed one of them communicate with his buddies about her looks, rating her nine out of ten. The detective observed the others sign lewdly amongst themselves as they ascribed ratings of their own. She stepped in front of the students, forcing them to pull up. Signing fluently, she asked, "Isn't it time you boys grew up?"

Surprised Valerie knew sign language, the students averted their eyes and sheepishly continued on their way. Only when certain they were no longer under her withering gaze did they resume their coarse signs.

Valerie spotted the lift doors and headed for them. En route, she was approached by a young, pimply student who had observed her arrival and somehow guessed she was something to do with law enforcement. In speech so garbled it all but hid his Devon accent, he asked, "Do you... knoww who... who da kil-ler is yet, Ma'am?" He couldn't hide his surprise when Valerie replied in flawless sign language, informing him her investigation hadn't even begun yet. He seemed satisfied with the answer and wandered off.

Valerie would learn later the lad she had just interacted with was one Dale Freemantle, a first-year student at Wandsworth. She'd have good reason to remember his name.

One of four lift doors opened nearby and its sole occupant, a young, uniformed cop, caught Valerie's eye. He'd been told to watch out for her. He motioned her over, and she hurried to join him in the lift.

Before the lift doors closed, they were joined by half a dozen students and staff members.

#

At that very moment, in the nurse's station adjoining the sickbay two floors above, resident nurse Jean Simons took the temperature of a somewhat flushed Carol Ashmore, another first-year student. Carol, a twenty-year old freckled redhead from Cambridge, had been feeling poorly all night. She coughed and sniffled as the matronly nurse removed the thermometer and checked it.

Concerned, Nurse Simons adjusted her surgical mask as she conversed with Carol in sign. "It's probably only a common cold, but I'd better take a swab."

A worried Carol could only look on as the nurse donned protective gloves and proceeded to give her a nasal swab.

After swabbing the patient, Nurse Simons transferred the swab to a viral container, which she placed in a biohazard bag together with a requisition form. The nurse then removed her gloves and signed to Carol that she would forward the swab to the nearest public health laboratory.

SILENT FEAR is available as a paperback and Kindle ebook via *Amazon.*

Other Books
by Lance & James Morcan published by Sterling Gate Books

HISTORICAL FICTION:

White Spirit (A novel based on a true story)

Into the Americas (A novel based on a true story)

World Odyssey (The World Duology, #1)

Fiji: A Novel (The World Duology, #2)

CONSPIRACY THRILLERS:

The Ninth Orphan (The Orphan Trilogy, #1)

The Orphan Factory (The Orphan Trilogy, #2)

The Orphan Uprising (The Orphan Trilogy, #3)

CRIME THRILLERS:

Silent Fear (A novel inspired by true crimes)

The Heathrow Affair

ACTION-ADVENTURE:

High Country Contract

The Dogon Initiative (The Deniables, Book 1)

NON-FICTION:

DEBUNKING HOLOCAUST DENIAL THEORIES: Two Non-Jews Affirm the Historicity of the Nazi Genocide

THE ORPHAN CONSPIRACIES: 29 Conspiracy Theories from The Orphan Trilogy

GENIUS INTELLIGENCE: Secret Techniques and Technologies to Increase IQ (The Underground Knowledge Series, #1)

ANTIGRAVITY PROPULSION: Human or Alien Technologies? (The Underground Knowledge Series, #2)

MEDICAL INDUSTRIAL COMPLEX: The $ickness Industry, Big Pharma and Suppressed Cures (The Underground Knowledge Series, #3)

THE CATCHER IN THE RYE ENIGMA: J.D. Salinger's Mind Control Triggering Device or a Coincidental Literary Obsession of Criminals? (The Underground Knowledge Series, #4)

INTERNATIONAL BANKSTER$: The Global Banking Elite Exposed and the Case for Restructuring Capitalism (The Underground Knowledge Series, #5)

BANKRUPTING THE THIRD WORLD: How the Global Elite Drown Poor Nations in a Sea of Debt (The Underground Knowledge Series, #6)

UNDERGROUND BASES: Subterranean Military Facilities and the Cities Beneath Our Feet (The Underground Knowledge Series, #7)

VACCINE SCIENCE REVISITED: Are Childhood Immunizations As Safe As Claimed? (The Underground Knowledge Series, #8)